"Alexis said she wanted to meet with me about one of the studies. We record all of those sessions with our volunteers. So if something strange happened with one of them, it ??? ?? the security footage."

The weight of Elliot's gaze warmed Waylynn's neck and face. Her pulse quickened. Her body surged to attention when he looked at her like that—like she was the only woman in the entire world—and her brain checked out temporarily. This place, the location, it suited him. If anything, he seemed more relaxed here than he had in the year she'd known him as her next-door neighbor. Fewer tension lines bracketed the edges of those gray eyes. If she was being honest with herself, in his tiny cabin, out in the middle of the woods trying to keep her safe, he'd never been more attractive.

"You want to be caught at yet another crime scene tied to this case? That's a terrible, horrible, incredibly foolish idea." He stood, clapping his hands together. "Let's do it and see what happens."

RULES IN
DEFIANCE

NICHOLE SEVERN

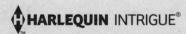

This one's for you!
Thanks for joining the Blackhawk Security adventure.

ISBN-13: 978-1-335-60479-8

Rules in Defiance

Copyright © 2019 by Natascha Jaffa

Recycling programs for this product may not exist in your area.

This edition published by arrangement with Harlequin Books S.A.

For questions and comments about the quality of this book, please contact us at CustomerService@Harlequin.com.

Printed in U.S.A.

Nichole Severn writes explosive romantic suspense with strong heroines, heroes who dare challenge them and a hell of a lot of guns. She resides with her very supportive and patient husband, as well as her demon spawn, in Utah. When she's not writing, she's constantly injuring herself running, rock climbing, practicing yoga and snowboarding. She loves hearing from readers through her website, www.nicholesevern.com, and on Twitter, @nicholesevern.

Books by Nichole Severn

Harlequin Intrigue

Rules in Blackmail
Rules in Rescue
Rules in Deceit
Rules in Defiance

Visit the Author Profile page at Harlequin.com.

CAST OF CHARACTERS

Elliot Dunham—He's set one rule for himself: no romantic attachments. But this Blackhawk Security private investigator soon becomes all that stands between the girl next door and certain death.

Waylynn Hargraves—Her entire life's work is put at risk when her assistant turns up dead in her bathtub. Waylynn's been accused of murder before, but the only one who can help her this time is the best friend she can't risk losing.

Alexis Jacobs—Waylynn's assistant has uncovered a dark secret within Waylynn's genetic research and threatens to reveal the truth, but someone has already made sure she'll never get the chance.

Kate Monroe—Blackhawk Security's psychological profiler.

Vincent Kalani—Blackhawk Security's forensics expert.

Chapter One

An ear-piercing scream had Elliot Dunham reaching for the Glock stashed under his pillow. He threw back the sheets and pumped his legs hard, not bothering to check the time as the apartment blurred in his vision. That scream hadn't come from his apartment, but close by. Air rushed from his lungs as adrenaline burned through his veins. There was only one name that came to mind. "Waylynn."

Ripping open his front door, he made the sharp turn to his left in the darkness and faced his next-door neighbor's front door. No hesitation. He aimed the heel of his foot toward the lock and kicked with everything he had. Pain shot up his leg, but the door frame splintered, thick wood slamming back against the wall. Dust flew into his beard and face as he raised the gun and moved in. One breath. Two. Nothing but the pounding of his heartbeat behind his ears registered from the shadows. He scanned the scene, his senses adjusting slowly.

He'd gone into plenty of situations like this before, but this wasn't just another one of his clients. This was Waylynn. She mattered. He'd trained out of Blackhawk Security, offered his clients personal protection, home security and investigative services, as well as tactical training, wilderness survival and self-defense. But none of that would do Elliot a damn bit of good now. He was running off instinct. Because when it came to that woman, he couldn't think. Couldn't breathe.

Debris cut into his bare feet as he moved deeper into the dark apartment. A broken picture frame— Waylynn's doctorate degree from Texas A&M University—crunched beneath his weight. Torn couch cushions, a broken vase, a purse that'd been dumped over the floor. Signs of an obvious struggle littered the living room, but it was the trail of dark liquid leading to the back bedroom that homed his attention to the soft sobs echoing down the hallway. Blood. "Waylynn? It's Elliot. Are you dead?"

"Don't come in here!" That voice. Her voice.

"I take it that's a *no*." While his gut twisted at her hint of fear, relief spread through him. She was alive. And the scream… Something horrible had happened to make her scream like that. The front door had been locked. No breeze came through the apartment from a broken window. Elliot moved down the hallway, putting the survival skills ingrained into him since he was fourteen to good use. No sign of a break-in. No movement from an intruder. He hit the bedroom and pushed the partially open door open with his free hand. The bed had been perfectly made, brightly colored throw pillows straight. Not much damage in this room. Light from beneath the closed bathroom door stretched across the beige carpeting.

And Elliot froze.

The gun faltered in his grip as water seeped from beneath the bathroom door. Not just water. Water mixed with blood. He shot forward. "I don't care if you're naked, Doc. I'm coming in."

Elliot shouldered his way into the brightly lit bathroom and caught sight of his next-door neighbor huddled against the wall. Ice worked through him as he took in her soaked long blond hair, her stained oversize sweater and ripped black leggings, the terrified panic in her light blue eyes as she stared up at him, openmouthed.

And at the dead woman in the bathtub.

"Oh, I didn't realize this was a party." A hollow sensation carved itself into the pit of his stomach as he dropped the gun to his side. Terror etched deep lines around her mouth. Pressure built behind his sternum. Elliot set the gun on the counter and crouched in front of her, hands raised. Mildly aware he wore nothing but a pair of sweatpants, he ignored the urge to reach out for her. He'd take it slow. The woman in front of him wasn't the one he'd moved in next door to a year ago. This wasn't the woman who'd caught his attention with a single smile and a six-pack of beer in her hand when she'd made the effort to introduce herself to her new neighbor. This woman was scared, vulnerable. Dangerous.

"Who's your friend?" he asked.

Her gaze wandered to the body, far too distant, far too empty. Color drained from her face. "Alexis."

"Okay, then. First piece of the mystery solved." Elliot framed her chin between his thumb and index finger and softened his voice. He didn't have a whole lot of training when it came to trauma victims, but he couldn't keep himself from touching her. "Second question. Are you the one bleeding?"

"I'm…" She turned that ice-blue gaze back to him, her voice dropping into hollow territory. "I'm not the one bleeding."

"Now we're getting somewhere." He lowered his hand, careful of where he stepped, careful not to leave prints. He'd barged into the middle of an active crime scene. A crime scene where the most trusting woman he'd known stood in the center. There'd been a struggle, that much was clear. Things had obviously gotten out of hand, but he needed to hear the rest from her. He'd learned to trust his instincts a long time ago and something about the scene, about Waylynn's scream a few minutes ago, didn't sit right. He pointed to the bathtub. "Last question. Why is there a dead woman in your tub?"

"I don't remember. It's all a blur. I woke up face-down on the bathroom floor. Water and—" she shuddered, wrapping her arms tighter around her middle "—blood were spilling over the edge of the bathtub. I got up and then I saw her. I screamed." Tears streamed down her cheeks and she wiped at them with the back of her long, thin fingers. She worked to swallow, her knees pressed against her chest, hands shaking. She blinked against the brightness of the lighting. "It's Alexis. Alexis Jacobs. She's my assistant at the lab."

Genism Corporation's lab. The largest, most profitable biotech company in Alaska. Also one of the military's biggest prospects for genetic testing, from what he'd learned, because Dr. Waylynn Hargraves herself had put them on the map. Advancing their research by decades according to recent publicity, she'd proved the existence of some kind of highly contested gene.

Elliot scanned the scene again.

He dragged his thumb along her cheekbone, focused entirely on the size of her pupils and not the fact every hair on the back of his neck had risen at the feel of her. Only a thin line of blue remained in her irises, which meant one of two things in a room this well lit. Either Waylynn had suffered a head injury during an altercation or she'd been drugged. Or both. He scanned down the long column of her throat. And found exactly what he was looking for. A tiny pinprick on the left side of her neck. The right size for a hypodermic needle. He exhaled hard. Damn it. She'd been drugged, made to look like she'd murdered her assistant. Framed. "What's the last thing you remember?"

Anything to give them an idea of who'd done this. Because it sure as hell hadn't been Waylynn.

She blinked against the bathroom lights as though the brightness hurt. "I... I was supposed to meet Alexis here, at my apartment. She said she'd found something alarming in the recent study I oversee at work, but she didn't want to discuss it over the phone or at the lab. She insisted on somewhere private where we couldn't be overheard."

If Waylynn headed that study, anything alarming her assistant uncovered would've fallen back on her, threatened the project. But not if Alexis disappeared first. Whoever'd killed the assistant had known she and Waylynn were meeting and planned the perfect setup. Pinning his next-door neighbor as a murderer.

"Okay. You had a meeting scheduled here," he said. "You obviously got in your car and left the lab. Then what?"

"I...don't remember." She wrapped long fingers around his arms. "Elliot, why can't I remember?"

"Sorry to be the one to tell you this, Doc, but I think you were drugged." He pointed at the faint, angry puckering of the skin at the base of her throat to distract himself from the grip she had around his arms. "Hypodermic needle mark on the left side of your neck."

"There're only a handful of sedatives that affect memory. Benzodiazepines mostly. We store them at the lab." Hand automatically gravitating to the mark, she ran her fingertips over the abrasion. Her bottom lip parted from the top, homing his attention to her mouth. That wide gaze wandered back to the tub and absolutely destroyed her expression. Waylynn worked over sixty hours a week at the lab. Stood to reason her assistant did, too. They'd probably spent a lot of time together, gotten close. Shock smoothed the lines around her eyes. Her hands shook as she covered her mouth. "But drugging me doesn't explain how Alexis... This can't be happening. Not again."

Again? Alarm bells echoed in his head and his fight instinct clawed through him. "You know, that makes me think you killed somebody in a past life I don't know about."

Movement registered from somewhere inside the apartment and Elliot reached for the gun on the counter. The metal warmed in his hand as he barricaded the door with his back.

Voices thundered through the apartment. Then footsteps outside the bathroom door. "Anchorage PD! We received a disturbance call from one of your neighbors. Is anyone here?" a distinct feminine voice asked.

"I don't know about you, but I haven't had this much excitement since getting shot at a few months ago." This night was getting better by the minute, yet Waylynn hadn't moved. "I don't mean to alarm you, Doc, but I think the police are here. And they're probably going to arrest you."

"Elliot, I think I killed her." Waylynn's fingernails dug into his arms harder. "I think I killed Alexis."

THIS COULDN'T BE HAPPENING. Not again. She couldn't go through this again.

Waylynn Hargraves pressed her elbow into the hard metal table, threading her fingers through her hair. Focus. She hadn't been charged with anything. Yet. They'd taken her blood to run a tox screen, but if Anchorage PD believed she'd killed Alexis, wouldn't they have put her in cuffs? She couldn't have killed her lab tech. She'd never hurt Alexis. They were friends. Even if… No. She'd been drugged. She'd been forced. Framed. All she had to do was remember.

Pain lightninged across her vision and she blinked against the onslaught of the fluorescent lighting above. A dull ache settled at the base of her skull. Whatever drug she'd been injected with still clung to the edges of her mind, kept her from accessing those memories. She couldn't think. Couldn't remember how she'd gotten to her own apartment, if she'd talked with Alexis, how she'd—

Waylynn swallowed around the tightness in her throat and lifted her attention to the mirror taking up most of one wall in front of her. They'd left her alone in this room, but she doubted the room on the other side of that glass was unoccupied. The weight of being watched pressed her back against the chair. "Elliot?"

The door to her right clicked open. A female uniformed officer set sights on her. Past memories overrode the present and, for a split second, Waylynn felt like the fifteen-year-old girl accused of murdering her father all over again. Scared. Alone. Pressured to confess.

Tossing a manila file folder to the table, the officer brought Waylynn back into the moment. Long, curly brown hair had been pulled back in a tight ponytail, highlighting the sternness in the officer's expression. "Dr. Hargraves, sorry to keep you waiting. I'm Officer Ramsey. I have a few questions for you about what happened tonight."

"I know how this works." Waylynn shifted in the scratchy sweatshirt and sweatpants Officer Ramsey had lent her after crime scene technicians had taken her blood-soaked clothing as evidence. This time would be different. She wasn't a scared teenager anymore. She'd left that girl behind, studied her way through school, worked multiple jobs to pay for it herself, graduated with a master of science, landed a job with the top genetics laboratories in the country as their lead research associate. The work she'd done over the last three years for Genism Corporation would save lives. But the research community wouldn't see anything other than a murder charge attached to her name. "I'm not sure how much I can tell you."

"You do know how this works, don't you?" Officer Ramsey took a seat, sliding the folder she'd placed on the table across its surface. Waylynn didn't have to look at the contents to know what they contained. Her sealed records. "You've done this before. Are you sure you don't want your attorney present?"

Done this before. That wasn't a question. That was an accusation.

Her entire career—everything she'd worked for, everything she'd left behind—crashed down around her. A wave of dizziness closed in, but Waylynn fought against the all-consuming need to sink in the chair. No. This wasn't happening. She didn't kill her lab assistant.

"I don't have an attorney. Listen, my father wasn't a very nice man. So if you're looking for some sign of sympathy when it comes to his death, you're not going to find it, but I didn't kill Alexis." She set her palms against the cold surface of the table to gain some composure. "If you read the file, then you know I was acquitted. There wasn't enough evidence to convict me of my father's murder."

She hadn't been the one who'd killed him.

"But there is now." Light green eyes pinned Waylynn in place. At her words, another uniformed officer shouldered into the room, handing Ramsey a clear plastic evidence bag and another manila file. The policeman closed the door behind him, nothing but silence settling between her and the woman across the table. Officer Ramsey held up the evidence bag for her to see. "Do you recognize this?"

A piece of paper? "No."

"Really?" Ramsey set the bag labeled "evidence" flat on the table and slid it closer. "Why don't you take a closer look?"

Picking up the bag, Waylynn studied the blank

sheet of paper, not entirely sure what Officer Ramsey intended her to see. She flipped it over. A gasp lodged in her throat as a flash of memory broke through her drug-induced haze. Sharp pain as she held on to the pen. The barrel of a gun cutting into her scalp. The handwritten words fell from her mouth as she stared at the note. *Her* handwritten words. "Tell Matt Stover I'm sorry. I had to save the project."

What was this supposed to be? A confession? A suicide note?

"Crime scene technicians discovered that note on your nightstand. That's your handwriting, isn't it?" Officer Ramsey collected the evidence bag, still holding it up. "Your supervisor, Dr. Matt Stover, who you mentioned in the note, was very helpful in providing us samples."

A flood of goose bumps pimpled along her arms. That was why they'd kept her contained in this room for so long. They'd been buying their time. Dread curdled in her stomach. If someone had forced her to write that note at gunpoint, what else had they forced her to do? What else would the crime scene technicians uncover? "Handwriting analysis can't be used as evidence in court."

"Right. You've done this before. I keep forgetting." A placating smile thinned Officer Ramsey's lips, deepening the laugh lines around her mouth as she leaned back in her chair. She pointed toward Waylynn's throat. "Tell me about that mark on your neck. What'd you do? Shoot yourself up with saline to make it look like you'd been drugged?"

A pitiful laugh burst from between Waylynn's lips. "What?"

She couldn't be serious. Why would she drug—

"The tox screen we ran earlier on the sample of blood you gave us came back negative for any kind of sedatives or other drugs." Officer Ramsey folded her arms across her midsection. "I have enough to arrest you right now, Dr. Hargraves. The only thing we can't account for is the gun you used to shoot Alexis Jacobs. You worked with her, didn't you? For three years. So why don't you tell me what really happened after you lured your lab tech to your apartment to kill her and where you stashed the weapon?"

Alexis had been shot? But Anchorage PD hadn't recovered the gun. Waylynn couldn't focus. Couldn't breathe. The toxicology screen was negative, but why couldn't she remember anything after she'd left the lab? She threaded her fingers into her hair. This was insane. There was no way she would've killed Alexis. "Talk to Elliot Dunham, my next-door neighbor. He was there. He broke down my apartment door seconds after I woke up on the bathroom floor. He heard me scream. That wouldn't have been enough time for me to stash a gun."

"He's in the next room over, but I'm not stupid enough to believe anything that comes out of Elliot Dunham's or his team's mouths, Dr. Hargraves. I rely on evidence." Officer Ramsey leaned back in her chair. "All this evidence, plus the voice mail Alexis left on your phone, is telling me your assistant uncovered something in your most recent research trial for Genism Corporation. Something that would bring the entire study down. You killed her to protect yourself."

The interrogation room door swung open for the third time and Waylynn studied a single man carrying a briefcase. Early fifties if she had to guess, short, cropped blond hair, piercing blue eyes almost the same shade as hers. The tight fit of his expensive suit and white shirt accentuated lean muscle, but it was the sternness etched into his expression that raised the hairs on the back of her neck. "My client won't be answering any more questions. This interrogation is over. Dr. Hargraves, I'm Blake Henson. Your lawyer."

Waylynn straightened. "I didn't call a lawyer."

"Your employer keeps me and my firm on retainer," he said. "Dr. Stover brought me in after the police coerced him into handing over writing samples without a warrant this morning."

The less than enthusiastic tone in his voice slid through her, which she understood. Blake Henson was a corporate lawyer, not criminal. Maybe she should've called her own counsel.

"Dr. Stover gave us those samples voluntarily, but nice try." Officer Ramsey collected the evidence bag with the handwritten note and both manila file folders and stood. "But it doesn't matter. You're just in time. Your client is about to be arrested for murder one, counselor."

"Not without a murder weapon she's not. Everything you have is circumstantial at best. For all we know, Alexis Jacobs shot herself to frame my client and had someone else get rid of the gun." Leveling the briefcase parallel with the table, Blake Henson slid the leather across the surface and hit the locks. He extracted a single piece of paper and handed it to Officer Ramsey. "Regardless, Dr. Hargraves signed a nondisclosure agreement pertaining to the research she and the deceased perform for Genism Corporation. Any intellectual property Dr. Stover provided to this department wasn't his to give, and I'm afraid you don't have a judge in the state who will overturn that, Officer. Trust me, I checked."

Officer Ramsey read the document, then lowered it to her side. "You're suing the department?"

"Not yet, but if you insist on trying to charge my client of Alexis Jacobs's murder without evidence, my firm won't have any other choice than to take you and the entire department to court." Blake wrapped a strong grip around Waylynn's arm and lifted her from her seat. A rush of heavy cologne churned her stomach as he escorted her to the door. "You, of all people, can't afford that, Officer Ramsey."

Was her lawyer threatening an Anchorage PD officer? Before Waylynn had a chance to say anything, he'd directed her into the hallway, his hand still tight around her arm.

"Doc." In the blink of an eye, Elliot was there, and a flood of relief washed through her. Elliot with his handsome face, dark brown hair, strong jaw, broad shoulders and athletic build. Elliot, the only man she'd ever let give her a nickname that actually made her feel better whenever he said it. No cuffs. He hadn't been arrested, but his normally gleaming stormy-gray eyes darkened with an edge as his attention locked on her lawyer's hand. "There a problem here?"

Waylynn wrenched her arm out of Blake Henson's hold. "I'm not being charged. Yet."

"Thanks to me." Her lawyer switched his briefcase from one hand to the other, then offered his hand. "Blake Henson. Dr. Hargraves's attorney. And you are?"

"Me?" Elliot closed in on her, ignoring Blake's extended hand, his shoulder brushing along hers as though he intended to possess her. His clean, masculine scent dived into her lungs. He looked angry, which was odd considering her next-door neighbor usually went to great lengths to hide what he was thinking by layering everything out of his mouth with sarcasm or a joke. This wasn't like him. Too serious. Too...dangerous. "I'm her damn bodyguard."

Chapter Two

"You won't be able to go home. Police tend to frown on someone living in the middle of an active crime scene." Elliot pushed the SUV harder. The faster he got her to safety, the faster the knot behind his sternum might let up. He never looked for trouble, but he had no problem befriending it. And Waylynn Hargraves had been trouble since the day he'd moved in next door. The most recent example would be her dead assistant's body in the tub. And the fact he'd nearly torn a man's arm off and beat the bastard to death with it for putting his hands on her.

Not very professional. But the moment he'd seen Blake Henson's hand on her arm, it'd taken every ounce of his control not to kill the lawyer in the middle of Anchorage PD's station. Possessiveness unlike anything he'd experienced before had clawed up his throat and taken control. Nobody—not her lawyer, not the police, not him—touched Waylynn without her explicit permission.

"I remembered something." Exhaustion clung

to her words. The sweatpants and sweatshirt someone at the station had lent her hung off her narrow frame, but nothing could detract from her overall beauty. The light in her ordinarily bright eyes had dimmed over the past few hours. Finding a dead woman in your bathtub could have that effect on a person. "When Officer Ramsey was questioning me, she showed me a handwritten note, and I remembered writing it. Only, in the memory, there was a gun pressed to my head." Her voice dropped as she stared out the passenger-side window. "Somebody forced me to write it."

"You're being framed for your assistant's murder, but I have a sense you already knew that." Someone had been in her home. Drugged her. Forced her to do hell knew what. And he hadn't heard a thing aside from her scream. Right next door. Elliot strengthened his grip around the steering wheel as downtown Anchorage passed in a blur. Working for Blackhawk Security certainly had its benefits. Use of the company's SUVs, health coverage, an armory of weapons, not spending the rest of his life behind bars in the middle of nowhere thanks to the founder of the firm. None of it did a damn bit of good if he lost the closest person he had to a friend. Snowy peaks along the Chugach Mountain Range glistened in the sun as they headed east, and he pushed one hand through his hair. Even in the middle of June, Anchorage gave him the proverbial middle finger. He missed the desert. He glanced toward Waylynn, then back to the road as the signal ahead turned red. "Anything else?"

"Nothing. Whoever drugged me knew what they were doing. I can't remember what happened in my apartment and the drug didn't show up on a toxicology screen. I guess I'll take that as a win-win situation. I'm not sure I want to remember what happened." Color drained from her face as she leaned her head into her hand and her elbow against the passenger-side door. Disheveled blond hair slid over her shoulder as she shook her head. The weight of her attention fell on him, hiking his awareness of her—of her flowery scent—to an all-time high. Geraniums. Her favorite. But not just from the bottle. Almost as though the scent had become a permanent part of her over the years. Now he couldn't smell the damn things without thinking of her. "Why did you tell my attorney you're my bodyguard?"

"I know you, Doc." And not because it was his job to know. He'd spent the last year as a private investigator for Blackhawk Security, uncovering the secrets his targets hid from the world, declassifying documents for his own curiosity. Hell, he kept files on every one of his teammates. His former navy SEAL boss, Sullivan Bishop, and the fact he'd killed his own serial killer father, forensics expert Vincent Kalani and the accusations filed against him back in New York, their resident computer geek, Elizabeth Bosch—Dawson, whatever she went by now—Anthony Harris's classified missions for the army, and the saddest of them all, their psychologist, Kate Monroe. But digging into Waylynn's past had never crossed his mind.

The light turned green in his peripheral vision. Car horns blared for him to get moving, but he didn't give a damn. "You're a scientist. You've spent your entire life in search of the truth and there's no way I'm going to let you get yourself killed going after this guy on your own."

"My boss was right." She hugged herself a bit tighter and stared out the windshield. "You and I spend way too much time together."

"Or maybe Dr. Stover wants you all for himself." Couldn't blame the guy. Waylynn had a pull to her, a sort of gravity that was hard to fight. Even now, something about her urged Elliot to close the small distance between them, but he'd never cross that line. Not with Waylynn. She needed his help now and that was as far as it would go between them. Ever. He stepped on the accelerator, barely making it through the light. Her mouth parted as though she intended to deny it. "Trust me, Doc. Bosses don't usually call lawyers when their employees are being charged with murder."

Helping them escape out of an Iraqi prison was another thing.

"I think Matt is more interested in my research than what's under my lab coat." Fingers spread wide, a combination of passion and excitement controlled her hands as she spoke. She did that a lot—spoke with her hands and he couldn't do anything but pay attention. "The research we're doing is important. Have you heard of the warrior gene before?"

"Is that the movie about the boxer?" he asked.

"The warrior gene," she said. "Nearly every human being alive has a monoamine oxidase A gene, but, in several cases, individuals with low activity in that specific gene were found to have higher aggression in certain high-stress situations. It's a variant and has come to be known as the warrior gene. Identifying the subjects who possess the warrior gene has the potential to save thousands of lives a year. Active shooters could be stopped before they picked up a gun because they wouldn't be able to get one in the first place. Homicide rates would plummet. Army, navy, air force, the entire military would benefit from our research."

"What? No psychic telling you who to arrest before the vision comes true?" Elliot made a sharp right turn and floored the accelerator as they climbed Seward Highway's on-ramp. Couldn't take her to Blackhawk Security. Despite the fact its founder and CEO, Sullivan Bishop, had turned it into a fortress, Elliot wasn't willing to take the risk while the building was still under construction. It'd been five months since a bomb had ripped apart the conference room, but the best place for Waylynn right now was with him. "What you're talking about sounds like science fiction."

"It's not like that." Her hands fell into her lap as they left the city limits.

Greenery bled together in his peripheral vision, the sunlight glimmering off the Turnagain Arm waterway almost blinding. He hadn't chosen Alaska. If it were up to him, he'd have left a long time ago, but he'd keep his promise to his employer. He'd work off his debt.

"And, no, we don't have a psychic predicting violent events and the justice system would never convict a person of a crime before the actual crime was committed," she said. "But knowing who carries the gene will be a huge step forward in genetic engineering and protecting lives."

"What you're saying is everyone with the warrior gene will eventually snap when put in a high-stress situation." Elliot turned off the highway, throwing them deep into the middle of the Alaskan wilderness just before the Potter Creek trailhead that led into Chugach State Park. The property wasn't much and he'd bought it for close to nothing, but he could keep Waylynn safe out here. And that was all that mattered. "Good thing I'm prepared for the zombie apocalypse."

"Not…everyone. But, according to the studies I've done, it's a possibility." Her voice wavered on that last part and he narrowed in on the slight twitch on the left side of her mouth. A tell. Waylynn cleared her throat as a rush of pink climbed up her neck and into her cheeks. She tipped her chin up, studying the surrounding trees as the SUV climbed up the dirt trail. Waylynn Hargraves was hiding something. "Why are you helping me?"

She could keep her secrets. For now. As long as they didn't get him killed. Because he sure as hell wasn't the sharing type. Besides, he had ways of uncovering the truth. No matter how deep it was buried. Elliot pulled off the main road, driving deeper into wilderness. No one would find them out here. And if they did, he'd come prepared. "I don't think you killed your assistant. If you had, you would've asked me for help burying the body."

A smile overwhelmed the exhaustion in her features and, for a split second, Elliot couldn't take his eyes off her. He'd never been the type to stick around long. A month here, a few weeks there. He'd made some enemies along the way, but having Waylynn next door settled the restlessness singing through his veins most days. "You have experience with that kind of thing?"

Elliot leveraged his palm against the steering wheel and stretched back in the seat. "Did I ever tell you why I came to Anchorage?"

She shook her head as the SUV bounced over fallen branches and dead foliage. He made one last turn, forcing her to reach for the handle above her seat before he brought the vehicle to a stop and hiked it into Park.

"I ran a con that ended with me on the wrong side

of the Iraqi government." Reaching back behind her seat, close enough to get a lungful of her light perfume, he grabbed the duffel bag he kept stocked full of supplies and hauled it into the front. "Turns out being paid for assassination contracts you never intended to carry out constitutes fraud when the people paying you work for the government."

A weak laugh escaped from her lips as those blue eyes of hers widened. "You're not serious, are you?"

"My boss, Sullivan, was starting a security firm here in Anchorage. Needed a private investigator. I was recruited for the job." Elliot shouldered his way out of the SUV, hiking the duffel over his shoulder. He clamped his hand on top of the roof of the vehicle. "And by *recruited*, I mean he made a deal with the people who had me arrested and is forcing me to pay back the money I conned out of those nice killers until we're even. After that, who knows. Maybe my next project will be getting paid to bury bodies for people with your warrior gene."

"You don't strike me as a professional con man," she said.

"That's what makes me so good at it." He winked at her, a smile pulling at one side of his mouth, and motioned her out with a single nod. "Come on. I'll show you around."

Waylynn focused on their surroundings through his open door. He noted the exact moment she realized where he'd brought her as her mouth parted. "Please tell me you're joking."

He couldn't hold back the laugh rumbling through him and turned toward the dark green cabin. "Not this time, Doc."

A TINY CABIN.

Not an *oh-this-is-so-cute-and-perfect* cabin, but a real, featured-on-the-Travel-Channel tiny cabin in the middle of the freaking woods. Broken twigs and foliage crunched under her feet as she rounded the hood of his company SUV. Dark green paint chipping off wood planks, a single window above the shack-like door. She ran her fingers through her matted, blood-tinted hair, then cringed at the thought of what she might look like. He couldn't be serious. "Anchorage PD is going to charge me with your murder in the morning and I'm going to tell them it's because you made me stay here."

There was no way they could both fit inside this thing. No way they wouldn't run into each other in there. Waylynn swallowed hard. They'd been friends for over a year. Every night when she came home from the lab, he was there in his crappy camp chair with two beers and that damn gut-wrenching smile of his. She'd tell him about her day. He'd tell her about his most recent investigation, then they'd head inside to their apartments. Alone. But this? The idea there wouldn't be any barriers between them? It'd either destroy their friendship or push it to the next level. Either way, their relationship would never be the same if she stepped over that threshold.

"Well, now you're trying to hurt my feelings." Elliot offered her his hand, the other cinched around the duffel bag he'd extracted from the back seat. He was giving her a choice. Giving her safety if she wanted it. "It's a lot bigger than it looks."

His easygoing smile and confidence melted through her. Of course he had confidence. Wasn't that what *con man* stood for? She'd known he had a past. Everyone did. But could she trust him to keep her safe? Trust him to help her uncover who'd framed her for Alexis's murder? That was the question. Despite his revelation about the con he'd pulled in Iraq—a con that'd landed him in prison—her gut already knew the answer. Waylynn stretched out her hand, sliding her fingers up his palm. Rougher than she'd expected. Calloused, as if he'd been working with some kind of machinery or maybe out here in the woods. Desire exploded through her with a single touch, just as it had back at the police station. "It better be."

A breeze whipped through the surrounding trees, shaking them into a frenzy as Elliot reached for the door. He led her inside, a rush of heat dissipating the goose bumps pimpling along her arms. A combination of wood and spice wrapped around her as the main living space came into focus. She glanced toward him, unsure what to say.

"What'd I tell you?" Elliot released her hand, tak-

ing his body heat with him, and motioned to the un-
believably modern space with both arms wide. He
set the duffel bag on the floor, then collapsed backward onto the single couch, fingers interlaced behind his head. For as small as the cabin looked from
the outside, the layout worked well for the limited
space. A fireplace, complete with a stock of fire-
wood, lay dead ahead. Off to the left of that, a single
countertop with bar stools on one side and a kitchen
sink and stove on the other. No dining table. Not
enough room. A short hallway led to what looked
like a bathroom with a set of stairs leading to a space
on the second level. The one and only bedroom. The
decor fit the location. Wood, wood and more wood.
Just as she'd expect from any other cabin stashed
in the wilderness, but the granite countertop and
brightly colored accents brought the entire room
into the modern era. It suited Elliot. At least, what
she knew of him.

"And you thought this would be awkward." He
compressed his mouth against a smile.

Surprise pushed through her. "I never said that."

"You didn't have to." He swung his legs over the
side of the couch and pushed to his feet. Closing in
on her, he leveled that dark gaze on her and every
cell in her body responded. "I read people for a living, Doc. It's what makes me good at my job."

Heat flamed up her neck and into her cheeks. She
brushed a strand of blood-matted hair behind one ear
and fought the urge to cross her arms. What else had

he read about her? "In that case, I can't promise you I won't let you down when you look at me too closely."

"What are you talking about?" One distinct crease deepened between his eyebrows as he shifted his weight between both feet. "You haven't let me down."

"Someone is framing me for Alexis's murder." Waylynn interlaced her fingers. She used her hands to speak a lot of the time, but right now, all she wanted to do was close in on herself. To hide. From whoever'd killed her assistant. From the man standing in front of her who knew her better than any other person in her life, but she didn't want to lie to him. Ever. "This isn't the first time I've been accused of killing someone."

Seconds slipped by. Maybe a full minute. She couldn't read his expression, didn't know what he was thinking. Was controlling what others read in his body language part of being a con man, too? "Say something. Please."

Elliot ran a hand over his beard, tugging on the end. "Tell me what happened."

The same intensity she'd witnessed back at the police station consumed his expression. "I was fifteen. My father..." She pushed back the memories, but her pulse skyrocketed. "He deserved what happened to him. The cancer had already affected my mom, and police concluded she didn't have the strength to do what had been done, so I became the next logical suspect. They took me out of school, arrested me and attempted to try me as an adult, but in the end, I was acquitted. Not enough evidence. They couldn't find the gun that'd been used to kill him." The Beretta 92 pistol he'd kept stashed away in the linen closet of her childhood home. "Same as now."

That gut-wrenching smile overtook his stubborn expression, and she struggled against the gravitational pull she experienced every time he came around.

"What are the odds someone has been accused of murder twice in their life?" he asked.

"In my experience? High. Normally? Zero."

He stepped into her, setting her chin between his index finger and thumb as he had in her apartment. Her insides turned to molten lava. Hesitation gripped her hard as he studied her. "Whoever's doing this is counting on you taking the fall for Alexis's death." He released her, the tingling sensation spreading behind her sternum fading. "I'm not going to let that happen."

All she had to do was lean forward—just a bit— to press her mouth against his. What would he taste like? Feel like?

A dull ringing reached her ears. Waylynn blinked to clear the last few seconds from her mind. She rushed to retrieve her phone from the pocket of the grungy sweats Officer Ramsey had lent her. The screen brightened with the laboratory's number. "This is probably my boss. I should answer."

Elliot swept his arms wide and bowed before retreating toward the door and, just like that, the intensity in his body language disappeared. As though it'd never happened. "By all means, use whichever part of this room you prefer. I'll grab the gear from the truck."

She stared after him as he closed the door. A small burst of disbelieving laughter escaped up her throat. No. Nothing was happening between them. That hadn't been a connection. It'd been her body's automatic reaction to a stressful situation. She and Elliot were friends and she'd keep it that way. They didn't have a future together. There *was* no future with her.

The phone vibrating in her hand brought her back into the moment. She swiped her finger across the screen and brought it to her ear. "Dr. Hargraves."

"Waylynn, I can't believe it." Dr. Matthew Stoker's frantic tenor intensified the stress lodged between her shoulder blades. "The police were here at the lab. They wanted copies of your reports to match your handwriting—"

"It's fine, Matt." Waylynn ran a hand across her forehead. Dr. Matthew Stoker had been her boss for close to ten years. He'd given her the opportunity to conduct her research and convinced Genism's board of directors to fund her projects. He was on the path to put the lab on the map for genetic research all before he hit forty. The entire company depended on him. But getting dragged into a murder investigation threatened his promising future. "You were doing what you had to for the best of the company. I don't blame you for handing the reports over. I'm sorry they came to you."

"Don't worry about me. Are you okay?" Static reached through Matt's end of the line. Or was that the sound of broken glass in the background? "I called the company lawyer for you. Blake Henson told me you'd been arrested, but they couldn't keep you in custody. Where are you?"

"I'm…" She didn't know what to say. She'd found her assistant dead in her bathtub and all the evidence Anchorage PD had recovered pointed at her. Someone had framed her for murder and the only reason she'd come out into the middle of the woods with Elliot was for her own protection. Should she trust Matt with the location?

The front door clicked open.

Elliot hauled another duffel bag inside, tossing it onto the floor, and her awareness of him rocketed to an all-time high. The zip-up hoodie he wore did nothing to hide the bulk in his arms and across his chest. The air in her lungs stilled. She'd never noticed his physique before.

What had changed?

"Waylynn?" Matt asked over the line.

She took a deep breath to restart her system as Elliot maneuvered around her in the small space and headed for the back of the cabin. His clean, masculine scent worked deep into her lungs, became part of her, and she had the feeling that was only the beginning as she studied the rest of the tiny space. He'd brought her here to keep her safe from whoever'd killed Alexis, but what if it was him who needed protection from her? "I'm somewhere safe."

"Good. Keep it that way, because there's something you should know." The tension in Matt's voice failed to drown out the tinkling of shattered glass over the line. "Someone broke in to the lab. Somehow a fire broke out and… Everything, all of your research from the past ten years… It's gone."

Chapter Three

"Good news. I found an unopened box of peanut butter Oreos stashed under the bed." He tossed the package a few inches into the air, then caught it. Her favorite guilty pleasure. Elliot pounded down the small set of stairs and rounded the corner into the main living space from the back of the cabin.

The color had left Waylynn's cheeks, her knuckles white around the phone in her hand. The hairs on the back of his neck stood on end at the sight of her. Forget the cookies. Tossing the package onto the counter, he pulled the weapon from his shoulder holster beneath his sweatshirt and clicked off the safety, ready for war. "Tell me whose ass I need to kick."

"Somebody doesn't just want to frame me for Alexis's murder. They're destroying my life." Her voice barely reached across the small space. Confusion deepened the color in her ocean-blue gaze. "Elliot, my research… It's gone. Everything I've worked for—for the past ten years, is gone."

His gut tightened. Hell. That'd been her life's

work, her career. And it was gone? Elliot didn't believe in coincidences. First, her assistant's murder in Waylynn's apartment. Now this. She was right. Whoever'd set her up to take the fall was ensuring she'd never get back up. He scanned the perimeter from the nearest window, then centered back on her, approaching slowly, and lowered the gun. Locking on the phone still clutched in her hand, he holstered his weapon. "Who was on the phone?"

"Dr. Stover. Someone broke in to the lab. There was a fire." Her voice hollowed. She somehow went even paler. Her attention snapped up as he closed the distance between them and everything inside him heated. The delicate column of her throat flexed on a swallow. "The fire department thinks it was arson. There were traces of accelerant all over my desk. Chemicals we keep in the janitorial closets."

He denied the urge to wrap her in his arms. While he hadn't taken her on as an official client—yet—the same rules applied. No getting involved with clients. "Just yours?"

She nodded but refused to let go of that damn phone. "Yes. Someone burned it all. My handwritten notes, my digital files, a decade's worth of studies and genetic testing… It was all in my desk or on my computer. What am I going to do?"

"What about a backup?" There had to be something salvageable.

"Genism doesn't allow employees to have backups other than the company server, but Matt said that's been tampered with, too." She swiped at her face, shoulders rising on a deep inhale as though her emotional reservoir had run dry. "We can't bring any foreign devices into the lab, take files out or save them to the cloud."

Of course they couldn't. That would make too much sense. And, suddenly, Elliot couldn't keep his distance from her any longer. Reaching for her, he slid his fingers up her arms. Calluses caught on her smooth skin, the rush of the scent of geraniums was intoxicating. "Waylynn, I'm sorry. I know how much your work meant—means—to you."

It was her entire life, her career. Her ticket out of a rough childhood, which he'd most recently learned included a murder accusation. She'd moved on from that life, had obviously worked hard for it. College, graduate school, becoming one of the foremost experts in the country on genetics. And in the flash of a flame, it was gone. Didn't seem fair.

"Does this place have a shower?" she asked.

"Bathroom is past the kitchen on the right." Elliot hiked a thumb over his shoulder and turned slightly to give her a line of sight. Despite the bloody tint to her blond hair, the smear of her eyeliner and mascara, and the fact she'd lost everything that mattered to her, Waylynn held her head high.

"Take your time. Clean towels are hanging behind the door," he said.

A single nod was all he got in response as she pulled out of his grasp and headed toward the bathroom.

The lock clicked into place and he didn't waste any time. Whoever'd framed her for murder had started the fire in her lab. He was sure of it. The timing. The opportunity. They both lined up. The SOB might be dangerous, but Elliot was worse. Because they'd never see him or his team coming.

Extracting his laptop from one of the black duffel bags on the couch, he flipped it open and took a seat at the counter. Framing Waylynn to cover up a murder was one thing. Alexis's murder could've had nothing to do with Waylynn, but his next-door neighbor happened to make the perfect scapegoat with her sordid past. Coming after Waylynn's research? That was personal. Someone was hunting her.

The unsub—unknown subject—had to know about her father's murder accusation in order for the frame job to stick. Except those records had been sealed because Waylynn had been a minor at the time. Which meant the bastard was either connected to the case or had premeditated pinning the murder on Waylynn by looking for something incriminating. He couldn't discount any possibility. Not when it came to keeping her alive.

Elliot glanced toward the bathroom at the sound of water hitting tile. It'd take a few minutes for her to wash off the blood. Focusing on the screen, he pulled up the internet browser and typed in her name. His finger hovered over the enter key. Of all the people he'd investigated, of all the chances he'd had to dig into her past, he'd kept Waylynn's off-limits, respecting her privacy. He had an entire team of coworkers. Former SEALs and Rangers, an ex-National Security Agency consultant, a military investigator, Blackhawk Security's forensics expert and a psychologist. He'd worked with them for over a year, trusted them with his life, but Waylynn was different. Special. Forbidden.

And yet someone was trying to hurt her.

He hit the button. The screen brightened as headlines filled the page. Top stories included the massive progress she'd made in the bioengineering community, but one stood out among the rest. "Rhinebeck, NY, fifteen-year-old acquitted of father's murder." Elliot read through the article. Waylynn had spent over three weeks in county lockup after her arrest on school grounds. Never gave a statement, never tried to blame the crime on someone else, or offered an alibi. Police had questioned her cancer-stricken mother at the time, but ultimately concluded Nora Hargraves didn't have the strength to lift the missing handgun used to kill her husband in cold blood. Without the murder weapon, the prosecution had no other choice than to release the teen despite ample motive and opportunity. Her mother had died during the trial.

Hell. In the year they'd been neighbours, he'd known Waylynn had lost her mother when she was younger, and about the foster family who'd taken her in until she'd turned eighteen, but he hadn't realized the circumstances. Elliot leaned back in his chair to break up the tightness in his throat. He'd been on his own since he was fourteen. Voluntarily. Waylynn had everyone taken from her in a three-week span. He glanced toward the bathroom.

But none of this narrowed down a suspect pool. Nathan Hargraves had been shot nine times and died from massive blood loss. The forensic pathologist who'd signed the death certificate hadn't gone into more detail other than a final conclusion reading "homicide" and a note that reported a mere five dollars in cash had been found on the body at the time of the autopsy.

No other family. No friends who'd seemed too beat up about her father's death. No reason for someone to come after Waylynn. He'd have to do some more digging, but if Alexis's murder and the fire at the lab had anything to do with Waylynn's past, he couldn't see it. Which meant their suspect had learned about the trial, but only planned to use it to secure an arrest fifteen years later. Would've worked, too. If police had recovered the gun.

Elliot ran a hand through his hair, then rested his elbow against the counter. She hadn't told him any of this. In the year they'd been neighbors, she'd never mentioned her parents, her hometown, the fact she'd been in the foster system at the age of fifteen. Then again, how often had he talked about his parents? His hometown?

"All right, Alexis Jacobs, show me what you've got." He rolled back his right shoulder, working through the stiffness that still paralyzed the scar tissue around the bullet wound there. If the unsub wasn't connected to Waylynn's trial, then someone wanted the assistant dead for a reason. What had Waylynn said when he'd found her in the bathroom this morning? Alexis wanted to meet because she'd found something within the study they'd been conducting at the lab. But with all of Waylynn's research destroyed, he doubted the assistant's discovery hadn't been destroyed with it. He scanned through Alexis's social media pages. Three different sites. Hundreds of pictures. But this one… Elliot stopped scrolling and straightened. The redheaded beauty with freckles had taken a photo of herself a few days before her death, showing off what looked like a new tattoo of a *Q* with a heart on her wrist. The Queen of Hearts. But it was what was behind her that urged him to lean closer to the screen. A black external hard drive sticking out of the victim's purse.

"Bingo." Waylynn had said Genism didn't allow employees to back up their files on foreign devices, but what if Alexis hadn't followed company rules? He needed to get that hard drive.

The bathroom door clicked open and in his next breath, Waylynn rounded into the kitchen. Damn, he hadn't even heard her shut off the water. Hair still wet, she notched her chin level with the floor and curled her fingers into tight fists at her sides. Defiant. Strong. Sexy as hell.

"Well, don't you look nice when you're not covered in blood." Nervous energy exploded across his back as he closed the laptop, sliding it against the granite. She didn't need to see photos of the woman she'd found in her bathtub. Didn't need to know he'd looked into her trial. He drew his eyebrows together when she didn't respond. "You okay?"

"I want to know who's trying to destroy my life." Determination had cooled the day's confusion in her expression. The tears had dried, her jaw set, and she focused 100 percent on him. "You're a private investigator. I'm hiring you and your firm. Find out who did this to me."

"WE NEED TO get to my lab." There were plenty of monsters who knew how to play at being human. Which one of them had ruined her life? The possibilities were endless. Someone from her own lab. A rival geneticist. One of the volunteers from her studies. Her research into the warrior gene fulfilled her in a way nothing else had managed to for her entire life. She wasn't going to let that go. Not for anything. The person responsible wasn't going to get away with it. Waylynn settled back against the granite countertop, crossing her arms across her midsection. Then again, not all monsters did monstrous things. "Alexis said she wanted to meet with me about one of the studies. We record all of those sessions with our volunteers. So if something strange happened with one of them, it'd be on the security footage."

The weight of Elliot's gaze warmed her neck and

face. Her pulse quickened. Her body surged to attention when he looked at her like that—like she was the only woman in the entire world—and her brain checked out temporarily. This place, the location, it suited him. If anything, he seemed more relaxed here than he had in the year she'd known him as her next-door neighbor. Fewer tension lines bracketed the edges of those gray eyes. If she was being honest with herself, in his tiny cabin, out in the middle of the woods trying to keep her safe, he'd never been more attractive.

"You want to be caught at yet another crime scene tied to this case? That's a terrible, horrible, incredibly foolish idea." He stood, clapping his hands together. "Let's do it and see what happens."

Reality snapped her back into the moment and she pushed thoughts of him into a dark little corner of her brain where she prayed it'd never see the light of day again. "What?"

"First things first." Elliot pointed toward her and closed the space between them faster than she thought possible. His body heat tunneled through her borrowed sweats as he slid one arm around her. Her breath caught in her lungs, surprise paralyzing her in place. In the next moment, he'd retreated, handing her a package of peanut butter Oreos. "You need to eat, then sleep. In that order."

She blinked, staring at the unopened blue plastic package in her hand. Tiny cabin. Limited space. He hadn't been stepping in for an intimate moment or to help tame the chaos eating her up from the inside. Waylynn released the breath she'd been holding. Had she wanted him to? "You know my favorite flavor of Oreos?"

"Investigating 101." He leaned back against the opposite counter. "Everything you need to know about a person is in their daily routine, and you, my friend, bring home a lot of peanut butter Oreo packages."

A burst of laughter escaped from between her lips, because if she didn't have this small release, she feared she might fall apart. "You just happened to have a supply here?"

"I may have wanted to see what all the fuss was about." He crossed his arms, emphasizing the muscles across his chest, and his boots at the ankles.

She played with the back of her earring, scraping her thumbnail along the edge of her earlobe. "And?"

"And they're addictive." A bright widening of his lips played across his mouth as he blinked at her, and every cell in her body shot to attention. How was it, after everything that'd happened this morning, he could affect her like this?

"That's what I thought." Waylynn peeled back the sticky plastic in an empty attempt to calm the uncertainty ripping through her, took a cookie, then offered him the package. Nope. Not even the combination of chocolate and peanut butter frosting could erase the last twelve hours. Alexis was still dead and her career had gone up in flames. Another flash of her writing that note skittered across her memory. She fought to steady her racing pulse and forced herself to study Elliot as he bit into an Oreo instead.

The rest of the world fell away. The charges against her, the accusing tone in Officer Ramsey's voice, the fact police would probably want to speak to her about the fire, too. In this moment, all she saw was him. Elliot. Her next-door neighbor, her closest friend who she'd spent countless hours quizzing on horrible '90s country music lyrics by text message throughout the day. Which he knew by heart. The only man who'd been able to change her breathing patterns with a single look in her direction.

Elliot laughed, pulling her back into the moment. "I promise I'm not that interesting, Doc."

Oh, no. No, no, no. She wasn't going to go down that road.

"Excuse me. I need some air." Waylynn discarded the remainder of her cookie into the sink and put one foot in front of the other until she reached the front door. She had to get out of here. Away from him. If only for a few minutes to clear her head. The wood walls blurred in her vision as she escaped out the front. The rush of a cold Alaskan breeze beat against her as she closed the door behind her. Her heartbeat pounded loud behind her ears, the pressure behind her sternum more manageable the longer she kept the door between them. She ran a hand through her damp hair easily. No longer crusted with blood.

The sudden surge of desire she'd felt for him in

those heated moments drained. She'd kept her and Elliot's friendship casual for over a year, but now… Now she'd started imagining that smile in the morning after they woke up in the same bed. How his hair would stick out in every direction as he prepared her breakfast. How they'd have the rest of their lives to test each other's knowledge of bad country music. She shook her head in an attempt to dislodge the fantasy. They were friends. Nothing more.

A ring of trees surrounded the tiny cabin, weeds cleared approximately fifteen feet in each direction. Nothing but wilderness and blue skies as far as she could see, and a sense of peace settled over her. Elliot had certainly picked the perfect spot to get away from reality. When was the last time she'd gotten out of town, away from work, took a break for herself? Waylynn took in a lungful of crisp, clean mountain air.

Short answer? Never.

After the trial, after her mother's death, she'd thrown herself into investigating what had gone wrong. Why her father's behavior had changed so drastically in such a short amount of time with no sign of disease, no evidence of cancer, tumors, mental disabilities, no added stresses at work. Why he'd suddenly turned against her and her mother. The yelling, the fights, the physical altercations. In the end, she'd tried to tell herself it didn't matter. He'd gotten what he'd deserved, but what if it hadn't been his fault? What if, like those afflicted with any other genetic disorder, he hadn't been able to control himself?

Waylynn rolled her lips between her teeth and bit down to fight back the burn in her eyes. A simple blood test had confirmed her theory. He'd been born with a variant of the monoamine oxidase A gene. The "warrior gene." By disrupting the neurotransmitters dopamine, norepinephrine and serotonin, the gene predisposed carriers to more aggressive and violent behavior. While Genism and their military contractors paid her to take advantage of those specific behaviors, she'd spent every waking minute looking for ways to neutralize them. One success. That was all it would take to change the world. To change *her* world.

Maybe then she and Elliot could become more than—

A low vibration came from the tree line, raising the hairs on the back of her neck. Movement shifted the weeds and bushes to her right and her blood pressure spiked. She unfolded her arms. The vibration grew louder, harsher, a split second before thick, brown fur and four long legs materialized at the edge of the trees. Black eyes focused on her and Waylynn couldn't move. Frizzy hackles raised along the moose's back. No antlers. A female. But with her ears flattened against her head and nostrils flared, she was just as terrifying as the male of the species.

Waylynn raised her palms in surrender, taking a step back.

Another warning reached her ears and outright

fear paralyzed her in place. The creature's long, thin face dipped toward two smaller brown faces at her feet. Her babies. Newborn twins. Waylynn wouldn't hold up against a full-fledged moose charge. The damn tiny cabin wouldn't hold up against the mother defending those calves. "Elliot."

His name barely registered over the moose's low-pitched growl. With a couple of licks to the newborns, the mother refocused her efforts on keeping them safe. Waylynn lowered her hands slowly, sweat building on her upper lip. She fought to breathe around the fear clawing up her throat. Any sudden move, any attempt to escape, and the moose would charge. Licking dry lips, she tried to speak again. "Elliot."

"Don't move." Warmth flooded through her. He stepped inside her peripheral vision, so quietly she hadn't heard him come outside. As though he'd been able to feel her fear from inside the cabin and had come running. Elliot shifted in front of her, attention on the mother and her young. It was only after he'd moved between her and the moose that Waylynn understood what he was trying to do. He tossed an apple in the creature's direction. His voice leveled with reasoning. "Nobody wants your babies, Mabel. They look like a handful. So I'll make you a deal. You can have the rest of these apples, but you have to get them to go."

"I take it you two know each other?" Waylynn kept her voice low. She didn't dare look away from the cow protecting her young despite the fact all she wanted to do was run.

"We've met." Elliot notched his head back toward her slightly. "Mabel moved in around the same time I had the cabin built. Thing One and Thing Two there were born about two months ago, and she does not like the fact I vacation close by."

Mabel searched for the fruit, then brought her head back up, mouth empty. A rough exhale expanded the moose's nostrils.

"All right, Doc, she's not taking the bait, and it looks like we're in the middle of a standoff." Elliot rebalanced his weight between both feet. "When I give you the signal, I want you to run as fast as you can for the cabin. Don't look back and don't wait for me."

"What?" Waylynn took her eyes off Mabel. "I'm not going to leave you out here to take on a moose by your—"

A wall of muscle slammed her into the dirt. Her head snapped back against the ground; she couldn't see straight. He'd moved so fast she didn't have time to comprehend what'd happened until the beat of twelve hoofed feet faded into the woods. Mabel had charged, her babies had tagged along with her, and Elliot had tackled Waylynn to the ground. She struggled to breathe as he positioned his hands on either side of her, that damn gut-wrenching smile stretching his mouth thin. "That was fun."

His exhales skittered along her oversensitized skin and her heart fought to break through her rib cage in response. He'd saved her life. From a moose. "You and I have very different ideas of fun."

Chapter Four

He'd made mistakes.

Life didn't come with a set of instructions, but Elliot probably wouldn't have followed them anyway. Having her this close, in his home away from home, was a mistake. He'd been trying to save her from a life-ending stampede by Mabel and her calves but instead had gotten the up-close-and-personal Waylynn experience. Even four hours later, with her fast asleep upstairs in his bed, he could still smell her perfume on his clothing, remember the widening of her pupils as he'd looked down at her, feel the smoothness of her skin against the calluses in his palms.

He swallowed against the tightness in his throat. It wouldn't happen. Not now. Not ever. And most definitely not with her. Sure, they'd been friends for a while, but friends didn't expect or ask for commitment. Not in the same way a romantic relationship did. He'd spent the better parts of his life at the mercy of others. Never again.

The sun had leveled with the horizon hours ago,

yet light still poured in through the windows. Daylight at midnight. No better time than to plan their next move. His phone chimed with an incoming message. Swiping his thumb across the screen, he read Vincent Kalani's report. No hard drive recovered from Alexis Jacobs's apartment. The former cop and Blackhawk Security's current forensics expert had a relationship with the Anchorage police chief, which had gotten the team out of a lot of sticky situations in the past few months. Brothers in blue or something like that. But the missing hard drive triggered Elliot's gut instinct.

Someone was framing Waylynn for her assistant's murder. Either the unsub had broken into Alexis's apartment and taken the drive before police had a chance to search the place or the redhead had taken steps to make sure it would never be found if her employer came calling.

Only one way to find out.

Threading his arms through his shoulder holster, he glanced up toward the loft where Waylynn slept. No point in waking her now. If he found the hard drive, he'd bring it back here and they'd go through it together. If not, he'd have no reason to break the bad news. She'd been through enough. Elliot turned toward the door but slowed as the hairs on the back of his neck rose on end.

"You, sir, are a terrible bodyguard." That voice. Hell, that voice could move mountains. He'd recognize it anywhere, had memorized every inflection and tone.

"In my defense, you're supposed to be asleep and I was going to set the alarm." He turned toward her. Air locked in his lungs as she came down the narrow set of stairs. Long blond hair shifted over her shoulders, the muscles in her lean, bare legs flexing as she moved. Bright teal toenails reflected the flames crackling in the fireplace a few feet away. "Are you wearing my MIT shirt?"

"As nice of a gesture Officer Ramsey made by lending me her sweats so she could keep my clothes as evidence, I couldn't sleep in them. Hope you don't mind. I found it on top of a stack of shirts by the bed." She tugged on the hem but failed to make a damn bit of difference hiding all that perfect skin. "Although, not sure it matters what I'm wearing. When I close my eyes…" She folded her arms, accentuating the slight curves beneath his shirt, but not even that could distract him from the fear in those mesmerizing blue eyes. "I didn't know you'd gone to MIT."

She was avoiding the subject, the thing that kept her from falling asleep. He'd let her. For now. Everyone had their breaking point. And he had a feeling the frame job, the loss of her research—they were just the beginning.

"Mechanical engineering. Didn't last long." The dean tended to look down on students getting paid to take exams for their graduating class.

"Mechanical engineer. Con man. Private investigator." Waylynn stepped off the last step and rested her weight against the kitchen counter. "Which one of you is sneaking out of your own cabin in the middle of the night to follow a lead without me?"

Damn, she was good. "That would be the private investigator." He scratched at his beard. "You'd mentioned Genism doesn't allow employees to store their work on foreign devices, but I have a picture of your assistant with a hard drive in the background." He opened the door partway. "Want to see what kind of trouble we can get into?"

"That depends." She notched her chin parallel with the floor, the small muscles shifting in the firelight. "You're not suggesting breaking and entering, are you?"

"Give me a little more credit than that." His phone chimed with an incoming message. Elliot swiped his thumb over the screen a second time, then turned the phone toward her so she could read the message herself. "I have someone on the inside. He's already at the location. Are you in or are you out, Doc?"

Shadows fluctuated along the right side of her face from the flames, darkening the small mole beside the bridge of her nose. Waylynn rolled her lips between her teeth, unfolding her arms. "In."

"Is that what you're wearing?" As much as he hated the thought of her covering up all that smooth skin, she couldn't exactly walk around downtown Anchorage in nothing but his T-shirt and her underwear without drawing unwanted attention. "I mean, I won't argue—"

"In your dreams, con man." She turned on her heel and marched straight back up the stairs. A smile curled at the edge of his mouth as he caught sight of the delicate tattoo inked behind her right ear. A small double-helix DNA strand. He'd always attributed it to her work in genetics, but knowing now what he did about her family, about her father, maybe there was more significance in those sequences than he thought.

A few minutes later, Waylynn rounded down the stairs, dressed in Officer Ramsey's sweats once again, hair pulled back in a long ponytail, and his gut warmed. He couldn't take his eyes off her. He cleared his throat to counteract the rush of heat climbing up his neck. Didn't help. Even in a borrowed, stained pair of sweats, she was the most stunning, addictive woman he'd ever met.

"Ready to go?" She settled that ocean-blue gaze on him and the entire investigation disappeared to the back of his mind.

Wouldn't happen between them. Not now. Not ever. He'd been imprisoned long enough. First, due to his parents and his upbringing. Second, from actual prison in the middle of the hottest hell on earth and now contracted with Sullivan Bishop and Black-hawk Security. A relationship with the woman waiting for him to answer would commit him for life. Because she deserved nothing less. Elliot swung the door open completely, then withdrew his weapon as he faced the midnight sun as a precaution. "I'd say ladies first, but I'm the one with the gun."

"Such a gentleman." Waylynn took position behind him, the wild rush of geraniums still clinging to him after their close call with Mabel the Moose.

He led her toward the SUV, senses at an all-time high. He doubted whoever'd framed her for Alexis Jacobs's murder had followed them all the way out here, but he wasn't going to take the risk. Not with her.

Movement registered off to the left, past the tree line, and her long fingers latched on to his nondominant arm. Elliot slowed, trying to hear anything past the hard pounding of his heartbeat behind his ears. Not from the possibility of danger—he'd tear anyone who came close to her apart with his bare hands—but because Waylynn's touch had rocketed his awareness of her ever higher.

"Are we going to have to outrun a moose again?" Her question wisped against his earlobe.

Iridescent white eyes shifted in the bushes. Most likely a fox. A laugh vibrated through him. His nerves had run a bit too high for his taste. "Come on. I'm sure Mabel and the calves have had enough excitement for one day."

"They're not the only ones." She released her grip on his arm and moved to the passenger-side door.

They took the ride to Alexis Jacobs's apartment in silence. Tinted, bulletproof windows cast them into darkness and, despite the fact he could see her clearly in the front seat, Elliot felt her all around him. In her scent still imbedded in his clothing, to the memory of her pressed beneath him as Mabel charged. Hell, even the skin beneath his hoodie burned with memories of her touch.

He'd kept his distance, no problem, for the past year, but over the last twenty-four hours, she'd defied the single rule he'd set for himself when it came to wanting her. The only change? She needed him now more than ever and he'd been stupid enough to hide her in his own damn cabin while he hunted the bastard doing this to her. They hit the highway and headed back toward Anchorage, the combination of road and rubber pulling him back into the moment. Get control. Solve the case. Move on with their lives. That was it. They'd go back to the way things were once her apartment was cleared as a crime scene. He'd pay off his debt to Blackhawk Security and move on and she'd probably work the next decade trying to recover her research.

He squeezed his knuckles around the steering wheel for some semblance of an anchor. Who was he kidding? There was no going back. Waylynn Hargraves had worked herself beneath his skin a long time ago. Once he'd taken on her case, he'd known nothing between them would be the same.

Alexis Jacobs's apartment wasn't far from the cabin. Fifteen minutes, tops, but it sure seemed like an eternity before they hit the complex's parking lot.

"I need to make one thing clear before we go any further, Doc." Directing the SUV into a spot at the back, away from curious neighbors, Elliot pushed it into Park. He hung on to the gear shift. "I'll work this case, I'll find out who framed you for murder, who destroyed your research, no problem. I'll protect you with my life if I have to because that's what you're paying me for. We're friends, but that's it. I'm not interested in anything more."

Her arched eyebrows drew together. "Did I give you the impression I wanted more?"

"No." Which only made this easier. "Just making sure we're on the same page."

"Friends." Waylynn shouldered her way out of the SUV but turned back before she closed the passenger-side door behind her with a nod. "We'll always be friends."

"We doing this or what?" A mountainous shadow crossed in front of the SUV, arms wide. Vincent Kalani, all six foot six of him, closed in on the driver's-side door as Elliot stepped out onto the pavement. Blackhawk Security's forensics expert kept a relationship with Anchorage PD, which was the only way he and Waylynn were getting inside that apartment. And the only reason Elliot had invited the former cop along. "Generally speaking, you're not supposed to bring the client with you along for the ride."

Elliot extracted his black duffel bag all operatives were required to carry and swung his gear over his shoulder. Motioning toward Waylynn as she rounded the hood of the vehicle, he smiled. "Try telling her that. Waylynn, this is Vincent. He's the forensics expert on my team."

"Nice to meet you." She shook Vincent's enveloping hand. "Thank you for helping."

"I'm only doing this because Elliot promised he'd stop stealing my lunch out of the office fridge." The forensics expert collected a bag identical to Elliot's from the pavement a few feet away.

"Hawaiian barbecue is my favorite." Elliot winked at Waylynn, then hauled his Kevlar vest over his head and strapped it tight. He handed her an extra vest from his stash. "He still has his lunches made by his mom."

"Well, since you kept me waiting here for thirty minutes, I decided to take a look at the place myself." Clapping his hands together, the former officer widened his stance as Waylynn donned the protective gear. "Do you want the good news or the bad news first?"

Elliot crossed his arms over his vest, tugging one hand down his beard as he focused on his teammate. "Depends on how bad the bad news is."

"The seal is broken on the door," Vincent said. "Someone's already been here."

"Who would want to break into Alexis's apartment?" Anger was better than tears, better than grief, better than guilt. Somewhere, deep inside,

Waylynn suspected everything that'd happened to that poor woman had happened because of *her*. She didn't know why, didn't know who. She'd have to live with that fact for the rest of her life unless they solved her case. She studied Elliot's and Vincent's faces in the dim streetlamps peppered throughout the parking lot. "Aside from us, I mean."

"I can think of one person." Elliot hefted his duffel bag back into the SUV, then slammed the door closed, gun in hand. "Whoever wanted you to take the fall for her murder."

A shiver raked down her spine, shaking her shoulders, and Waylynn wrapped her arms around herself. "Could they have been looking for the hard drive, too?"

"They'd had to have known about Genism's policy to become suspicious if they saw the same photo as I did." Elliot pulled back the top portion of his gun, presumably chambering a round. She didn't know anything about guns. Didn't know why he needed one now, but the confidence rolling off him in waves helped settle her nerves.

The reality of his words cleared. She unfolded her arms and stepped into him. "Wait. You think someone from Genism is doing this to me?"

"I don't know. Seems too much of a coincidence. First, Alexis is discovered dead in your bathtub, then there's a break-in at the lab, where only your research is destroyed." His expression softened, but the intensity in his eyes remained. "I made you a promise,

Doc. I will protect you. Whoever is doing this might be dangerous, but I'm worse. Because they'll never see me coming."

A second shiver climbed along her back and it had nothing to do with the investigation or the danger closing in on her. For an entire year, she'd relied on Elliot Dunham's sense of humor to get her through the rough patches. She'd catch herself smiling at work when she remembered a joke he'd told a day earlier. Every night, after she left the lab, she couldn't wait to get home and find him in his cheap folding chair outside his apartment with two beers and that gut-wrenching smile so she could hear about his day. He had a gift and he didn't even know it. The gift to help her forget the nightmares. But the man standing in front of her wasn't the Elliot she'd known. His expression was harder, his voice dropping into dangerous territory, yet she couldn't stop the explosion of traitorous desire in her lower abdominals.

"I really want you guys to have your happily-ever-after—" Vincent hiked a thumb over his shoulder "—but we have an apartment to search before someone calls the real cops."

Waylynn blinked to clear her head and dug her fingernails into the center of her palms as a distraction. The heat rushing through her dissipated. For the moment. Her mouth dried. "We're friends—"

"She's my next-door neighbor." The tendons along Elliot's neck flexed. The sharp edge etched into his expression cut through her. He nodded once.

Oh. Disappointment wrapped around her heart and squeezed the air from her lungs. Next-door neighbor now? That was quite the demotion.

"Great. Then let's get going." Rolling his eyes, Vincent shouldered his duffel and led the way up the nearest set of stairs. The sound of the forensics expert's cargo pants shifting faded. She and Elliot were alone under the streetlamp.

"You should hang back, Doc. We don't know what we're walking into up there." He tossed her the keys to the SUV. "If I'm not back in ten minutes, drive to Blackhawk Security and talk to Sullivan Bishop no matter what happens. Only him, understand?"

She closed her fingers around the keys. What was he talking about? He was coming back. If he didn't... No. She didn't want to think about that.

Elliot turned his back to her, heading after his teammate with gun in hand.

"Is that really all I'm ever going to be to you during the investigation?" Her mouth dried, but she had to get the words out. She'd never been good at handling her impulses, couldn't stop herself from closing the small space between them as he slowed at the bottom of the stairs. They'd always kept things friendly. No romantic entanglements. But his pulling away from her now, after everything that'd happened? No. She needed him. Needed that damn smile, his sarcasm. His friendship. Because without it—without *him*—the chances of her fighting back the darkness that resided deep inside grew smaller every day. "Your next-door neighbor?"

He turned his head over one shoulder without facing her. "I can't do this with you right now, Doc."

"Vincent said someone's already searched the apartment. You think going up there in two minutes rather than one is going to make a difference?" She was part of the investigation, too. She *was* the investigation. She knew the risks, understood the importance of any evidence left behind in Alexis's apartment, or what would happen if she was caught here, but Waylynn needed an answer now. If this friendship couldn't handle the strain… She inhaled slowly to steady her pulse. She'd spend the rest of her life behind bars for murder. "We've been friends for almost a year. At least, I thought we were. We start working together and all of a sudden, you're pushing me away. I want to know why, Elliot."

"No, you don't." He started back up the stairs. As though that was the end of the conversation. "It would only make this harder."

They weren't done. Too much counted on his being in her life. Waylynn shot her hand out, wrapping around his arm before he could escape. "That's not good enough."

He spun around, closing in on her until he'd sandwiched her between his body and the side of the SUV. Despite the lingering sunset around them, his eyes burned bright. Every muscle in his upper body strained tight beneath his Kevlar vest as he bracketed his hands on either side of her head.

"You've been the one constant in my life. The one person I can count on to keep me here when all I want to do is get the hell out of this city." The tension drained from his shoulders, from his expression. His voice softened as he studied her, his body heat tunneling through her clothing. "But I haven't been free in a long time, Doc. I left the commune when I was fourteen, then spent over a year in an Iraqi hellhole until Sullivan Bishop pulled me out. Getting more attached to you than I already am? That puts me in a position I don't want to be in. So if looking at you as a friend instead of anything more helps me keep that distance, I'm going to do it." His hands slipped down the driver's-side door and he backed off. "I have to. For both our sakes."

She fought back the burn in her lower lash line. She wasn't a crier. She'd survived too much to break down every time something went wrong in her life, but this cut deeper than when she'd been accused of her father's murder, of Alexis's murder, of losing her entire life's work in the blink of an eye. This was Elliot. The only person she trusted. The only man who'd actually made her feel. Her friend. She swallowed to keep her voice steady despite the chaos battling inside her. "Then friends it is."

Her hands shook. One breath. Two.

"Vincent is waiting on us." Waylynn clenched her back teeth and everything inside her went cold. Circling around him, she headed for the stairs. He didn't want to be more than friends? Fine. She'd focus on the investigation, then move on with her life. With or without him. All that other stuff like relying on him to lift her mood with a joke or looking forward to that beer after she left the lab every night... Her throat got a bit tighter as she climbed the concrete steps. She'd get over it.

His boot steps echoed behind her, but she didn't dare look back to see how close he followed. Find the hard drive. Solve the case. That was all that mattered. Her life depended on it. She passed blue door after blue door on her right until the one with a broken crime scene seal came into view. Alexis's apartment. Waylynn pulled up short, not sure if she wanted to step over that threshold. Vincent had already gone inside. The sound of his search reached her ears.

Alexis Jacobs had worked directly under her for three years. Receiving and processing DNA samples from the studies they ran, recording their findings, running the needed tests to distinguish which of their subjects carried the warrior gene. Her work had been integral to the lab, integral to Waylynn. But it'd been more than that. Alexis had been a friend. They'd spent late nights together, ordering in Chinese food while they worked. They talked about each other's lives, love interests, vacations they wished they could take. Talked about Elliot. Alexis had been five years younger, but Waylynn had gotten along with her assistant better than most researchers her age in the industry. She took another deep breath and glanced back over her shoulder, a hint of bleach on the air.

"You don't have to go in there." His clean, masculine scent worked to drown the burn of bleach from her nose. Someone must've dumped an entire bottle in the apartment.

"Yes, I do." She needed to know why. Why the killer had targeted Alexis and not Waylynn directly. Why they were trying to set her up for murder. Why they'd gone after her research. Maybe whatever was on that hard drive would give her the answers. But most of all, she owed it to Alexis.

She pushed inside, covering her nose with the crook of her arm. Blinking back against the onslaught of chemicals, she searched for the black hard drive Elliot had described. The smell had soaked into the walls. They wouldn't be able to search the apartment long before it went to their heads. "Do police normally soak the place in bleach?"

"Not unless there's a body." Elliot covered his mouth and nose as well as he moved into her peripheral vision. Watching where he stepped, he moved toward the kitchen at the back through debris from a busted coffee table, an overturned bookcase, glass from picture frames. There'd been a struggle here. "Even then, they'd never leave the place inhospitable. Vincent, what you got?"

The former NYPD officer came around the corner, with a briefcase he must've stashed in his duffel bag. "Nothing. Place has been wiped down. No fingerprints. And I'm sure you didn't miss the fact everything's been soaked in bleach."

"We noticed." Waylynn used her sweatshirt over her hand as she pulled drawers and checked under unopened mail. No sign of the hard drive around Alexis's desktop computer. Nothing in her desk. She moved down the hall toward the single bathroom there. If Alexis had broken Genism corporate policy by loading private research onto a foreign device, she'd hide that hard drive the last place police or the company would find it. The last place a man would look. She centered her attention on Vincent. "Did you check the bathroom?"

"Checked the vents, the medicine cabinet, everything while you two were taking your sweet-ass time in the parking lot." Vincent shook his head. "No hard drive."

She didn't want to think about her conversation with Elliot right now. Finding the hard drive mattered. Clearing her name of murder mattered. Waylynn moved down the hallway and into the bathroom. Focusing on the blue-and-pink box beside the sink, she reached inside. Bingo. Pulling the solid piece of black plastic and metal from the thin cardboard, she stepped out into the hallway. She'd found the hard drive, and was holding it up for their inspection. "This is why you never send a man to do a woman's job."

Chapter Five

No identifiable fingerprints in the victim's apartment. Nothing to help them put a face to whoever
was gunning for Waylynn. The entire place had been
bleached down. DNA gone. Elliot exhaled hard to get
the chemical burn out of his nose. Didn't help. The
only lead they had now was the hard drive they'd
handed off to Vincent to give to Elizabeth Dawson.
In Liz's own words, Blackhawk Security's head of
network security would love to have something to do
other than change diapers and wash bottles all day.
But even checking in with his favorite teammate out
on maternity leave wasn't enough to pull Elliot out
of his own head.

He caught sight of Waylynn on the balcony, staring out over the parking lot, and closed the door
to Alexis's apartment behind him. Long blond hair
shifted across her back, but she didn't look back at
him. Hell. He'd messed up. Hurt her. Sliding his fore-
arms across the iron railing, he took a position next
to her. "You okay?"

"I am very not okay, Elliot." She intertwined her long, delicate fingers together over the railing and rounded her upper body, stretching back. Then she straightened, her bottom lip between her teeth. She unlocked her hands, then relocked them. "In the span of two days, I've lost everything. My coworker, my research. Now I'm losing you. All because someone put a body in my bathtub."

His gut clenched. Elliot turned toward her. "Doc—"

"The jokes. The sarcasm. I know it's a way to protect yourself, but you've gotten so good at protecting yourself, you're starting to push the people who care about you away." Ocean-blue eyes locked on him, full of fear, full of loss, and every cell in his body reacted. Because she was right. He didn't let people get close. She'd been the only exception, and even then he hadn't revealed a whole lot over the last year. It'd been the only way to survive. "Don't worry, Elliot. I got your message loud and clear." Waylynn turned from him, heading toward the stairs as she called over her shoulder. "I'll hire another investigator."

Like hell she would.

"No, you won't." Elliot shot his hand out, wrapping his fingers around her arm. He turned her into him and palmed the nape of her neck. Pure, unfiltered body heat worked through her clothing and down into his bones. She wasn't going anywhere. "Nobody else can protect you like I can."

"What are you doing?" Waylynn set her hands

against his chest but didn't fight to escape the circle of his arm. Her pulse pounded at the base of her throat. Wild, erratic. A sharp gasp left her mouth as he held her. Her exhales brushed across his face and neck. Mere centimeters separated her mouth from his. He should let her go. Let her hire another investigator. But he couldn't. Her geranium scent filled the space between them, chasing the bleach burn from his lungs, and he was lost. In her.

"You haven't lost me, Doc." Because a life without her in it wasn't a life at all. She was the only one keeping him in Anchorage aside from Sullivan's threat of hunting him down if he skipped out on his promise. The only one who'd made it possible to think about a future that didn't include four walls and a hole in the floor. "You never will, understand?"

"I don't want you working this case if it means we can't be friends after it's over." She licked her lips, homing his attention to her perfectly soft mouth. "You're… You're the only one I have left."

He released his hold on her and enfolded her in the circle of his arms, her ear pressed to his heart. At five foot eight, she fit perfectly against him. Setting his cheek against the crown of her head, Elliot breathed her in deep. And started humming.

"Are you humming 'She Thinks My Tractor's Sexy'?" Waylynn pushed away and pressed a single hand into his chest. She tried to hide a smile but couldn't fight it for long as she stepped back. "That's cheating. You know I love that song."

"You have horrible taste in music." Elliot took her hand, intertwining his fingers with hers, and led her into a spin beneath his arm. Calluses caught on her skin, but she didn't seem to notice. Or didn't care. Damn that smile. Damn what it could do to him, how far he was willing to go to see it one more time.

He kept up the rhythm and swung her into him. One hand on her waist, the other lifting her hand out to the side. In the midnight sun, he could make out the small bit of hazel circling her pupils. A light Alaskan breeze picked her hair off her shoulders, and in that moment, he wanted nothing more than to fist it in his hands.

"You never told me you grew up in a commune." Her voice softened.

"My parents were—are—very religious." As far as he knew, they were still alive, helping take care of the communal farm and property. Elliot swung her a full ninety degrees as a distraction. This stuff… He hadn't talked about it—hadn't thought about it—in over twenty years. "Up until I turned fourteen, farming, church and chores were all I knew."

"Was it just you and your parents?" She tilted her head to block the midnight sun from his face, the laugh lines around her eyes shallower than a few minutes ago.

"I have three sisters. Two older, one younger." Wow. How old would they be now? He didn't even know if they were still part of the community they'd been raised in. "Which means I learned how to braid hair, sew a hem and do my own laundry."

"Do you keep in contact with them?" Waylynn slid her thumb up the sensitive skin on the back of his hand.

"I haven't spoken to them since I left." His throat dried. The night he'd told his parents he was leaving was the last time he'd seen them. "When I was six, we had a guy come stay with us who had a brand-new— at least, new back then—Nikon F401S camera. It was the first piece of technology I'd ever seen." He could still remember that moment clearly. "I was so enamored with this thing, kept bugging the owner to let me see it behind my parents' backs, that he actually gave it to me when he left." Her favorite song faded to the back of his mind, but Elliot only pulled her closer as the past threatened to override the moment. "I took it apart piece by piece and put it back together to see how it worked. Worked great. I'd take pictures of the farm when I was supposed to be doing my chores, hide it under my bed at night until the thing finally died. I didn't have any way to charge it. That was when I knew there was more out there than the fences we'd built around the property." He shook himself back into the present. "So when I was fourteen, I left. And I haven't looked back."

"You've been on your own since you were fourteen?" Waylynn stilled. Soft, strong, beautiful, intelligent. He was a damn fool for getting this close. No matter how often he'd tried to deny it, this woman had a pull to her, a gravitational orbit he couldn't get away from. Didn't want to get away from. "How did you survive?"

Elliot cocked his head to one side. "Well, running cons helped. Until the Iraqi government wasn't afraid to call the local police in for me ripping them off for assassination contracts I never intended to follow through on."

A lithe laugh bubbled from between her lips and, for a moment, he forgot to breathe. "Now here you are. Learned your lesson, I hope?"

"For now." A smile escaped his control. It was impossible not to smile when she looked at him like that. Like she was happy. And considering the toll the past twenty-four hours had taken on her, he'd stretch this moment out as long as he could. Elliot dropped his hold on her waist and took a step away. To prove he could. His phone vibrated with an incoming message. "Vincent handed over the hard drive to our tech. And it looks like Anchorage PD released your apartment as a crime scene a couple hours ago. Maybe we can find you something else to wear besides those sweats and my MIT shirt."

Her blue gaze narrowed in on her assistant's apartment door, but she didn't drop his hand. "We're just going to leave all of her stuff? Alexis has some family on the East Coast, but I don't know anything about them."

"Once the police are finished with whatever they're doing in there, everything will be taken care of." Elliot ran the pad of his thumb beneath her signature mole beside her nose. The dark circles under her eyes hadn't budged. When was the last time she'd really slept? Over twenty-four hours ago? "Blackhawk retains one of the best lawyers in the country. We can have her get involved to make sure it all goes where it's supposed to if that's what you want."

"Okay." Waylynn nodded but didn't move when he started down the cement corridor. "We haven't solved anything."

He didn't have to ask what she'd meant. No, they hadn't. He'd deflected the hard questions by humming her favorite song and pulling her into him. But one thing had become clear: keeping her at a distance wouldn't work. Not as long as he was investigating her case. But he didn't trust anyone else to protect her like he could.

Elliot curled his free hand into a fist. Catch-22. Because the longer he stayed with her, the weaker his resolve.

She deserved nothing less than a best friend who'd never stand her up, reassure her when she felt insecure, comfort her after a hard day at the lab. Inspire her. Help her live without and forget regrets. She deserved a man who would give in to her most intimate desires and enable her to become the most confident, sexy, seductive woman alive. Even more so than she already was.

But he wasn't that guy. He couldn't be. Elliot locked his attention on the ocean-blue depths of her fear-charged gaze and his gut twisted. "I'll take a bullet for you if it comes to that, Doc. But that's all I have to offer."

THAT'S ALL I have to offer.

The words burrowed into her bones, dug in. Painful. Crushing. But she couldn't think about that right now, refused to acknowledge the hurt building behind her sternum. She had more important things to worry about. The fact someone had tried to frame her for murder, yet again. The fact she'd have to build her research from the smallest strand of DNA up. Again.

Waylynn stayed quiet on the drive to her apartment, but the fire traveling through her veins refused to relent. The soft, white iridescent glimmer of light from Genism Corporation across town held her attention as Elliot drove them through the city. Why? Why would someone do this to her? She'd moved on with her life, left the past behind. She clenched her teeth so hard her jaw protested. It was the only way to escape when the memories found a hole in her defenses. She glanced at Elliot in the driver's seat, his knuckles stark against the black leather of the steering wheel as they pulled into the parking lot of their apartment complex.

She exited the SUV without a word, didn't bother to check behind her to see if he'd followed. She didn't care. They were next-door neighbors as long as they were working together. He'd made that more than clear. But he was still her bodyguard. "I'll only be a few minutes."

Elliot's hand branded her upper arm as he hauled her into him, his touch burning through the material of her borrowed sweatshirt. Would she ever stop reacting to him like this? "You're not going in there alone, Doc. We don't know how deep this guy's connections run."

Doc. The word grated in her ears now. Where she'd normally taken comfort with the use of his nickname for her, she pulled out of his grasp. "Are you genuinely concerned for my safety because we're next-door neighbors or because I'm paying you?"

He interlaced his hands behind his head as a rough exhale brushed against her neck. Frustration deepened the divide between his dark eyebrows. "You are—"

"Beautiful," she said. "Intelligent, immensely talented?"

Faster than she thought possible, Elliot crushed his mouth to hers. Gripping her waist, he pulled her to her tiptoes and brought her closer. His arms caged her against him. The overload of desire rocketed her heart rate into her throat. He was all around her, the only thing keeping her upright when her legs threatened to slip right out from under her. She fisted his hoodie in her hands as the surprise wore off. He traced her bottom lip with his tongue and every nerve ending in her body fired in response as she gave him tacit permission to keep going with a slight nod of her head.

The air she breathed thickened, the investigation, Alexis's death, her torched career, were all packed into a tiny box in the back of her head as he kissed her. Kissed her as though he intended to devour her. His hands on her hips disrupted reality, helped her forget the nightmares. She never wanted it to end.

Elliot set her down, pulling away too fast. Too soon. "I was going to say *infuriating.*"

Her fingers ached as she uncurled them from his hoodie. Considerable muscle and strength lay beneath the thick layer, a warm vitality that urged her to press into him. Waylynn swiped the back of her hand across her lips, then stepped out of the circle of his arms. She'd had lovers. She'd gotten serious with a boyfriend in college, but she'd ended it the day she'd found out about her genetic heritage. But that kiss... Oh, wow. A kiss like that was worth the risk. A wave of dizziness blurred her vision and she blinked to clear her head. Her lungs spasmed for oxygen. She'd forgotten to breathe. "That was..."

"Extraordinary," he said. "Phenomenal, the best you've ever had."

"I was going to say *confusing.*" She took a deep breath as reality closed in. "I don't think you're supposed to kiss your next-door neighbor like that."

"You're right. I'm sorry." He shook his head, avoiding looking right at her as he backed off. He ran a hand through his hair, the butt of his gun visible as his hoodie shifted. "Small miscommunication between my brain and my mouth. It won't happen again."

"I'm going to go pack a bag." She headed for the stairs, hand on the chilled steel railing. "I'd prefer if you didn't follow me."

Waylynn exhaled his clean, masculine scent from her system, not caring if she'd offended him. She needed space, a few minutes to clear her head. Maybe that was the problem. She couldn't think when he touched her, not when he helped her forget there was a monster out there intent on destroying everything she cared about. She swallowed back the urge to rub at her sternum as the hurt set in. Climbing the stairs to the second level of the apartment complex, she deflated. The worst part about this whole thing? She couldn't even blame her lack of resistance on lust alone. Elliot had burrowed beneath her skin, become part of her, long before tonight. She just hadn't wanted to see the truth: a relationship between them couldn't work. Not when her genetic makeup fated her to turn on him at the drop of a hat.

Stretching her hand toward the sconce bolted beside her door, she unscrewed the ornate bottom loose and caught the key hidden inside. She slipped the key into the lock, but the door swung open on its own. The rush of a combination of cleaning supplies and sweat lingered on the air. Her stomach churned. Pulling the key from the door, she remembered the crash of wood against drywall as Elliot had forced his way inside to get to her. Her apartment had been a safe haven, somewhere to wash off the pressure of the lab and pamper herself every night after she left him on the porch with a half-finished beer. But now… Waylynn closed the door behind her, back pressed against damaged wood. Too many other people had been here. Alexis. Her killer. Elliot. The police. It didn't feel like home anymore. Didn't smell like it either.

Pack a bag. Find the person responsible for ruining her life. She wouldn't break now. She was a survivor. "You've been through worse."

Waylynn pocketed the key in her hand and headed straight through the living room to the hallway. She'd made it only a few steps when pain seared through her skull, unbalancing her, and she collapsed against the wall. Hand on her forehead, eyes closed tight, she couldn't stop the sudden rush of memory pounding at the back of her head. Her pulse sped up, lungs working overtime.

Tall male. Light brown hair, maybe blond in the dim lighting. A scar on the back of his right hand as he pressed the gun to her temple. He'd forced her to write the confession. The gunshots echoed in her ears as though there was someone shooting right beside her. Three suppressed pulls of the trigger. Alexis's eyes widened in surprise, then emptied of life right in front of her. He'd killed Alexis. He'd framed Waylynn for the murder. *You're not going to remember any of this.*

"Waylynn." Rough hands shook her back into the present.

She gasped, kicking as her fight-or-flight instinct engaged. Waylynn wedged her heels into the slightly damp carpet to escape but didn't get far before she recognized that voice. *His* voice.

"Doc, it's me. You're safe. I'm not going to hurt you." He stood, palms raised in surrender, not daring to approach. Elliot crouched in front of her and rubbed one hand into his stomach. "Damn, you've got some powerful legs."

"Elliot." She automatically studied the back of his right hand as he draped it over one knee. No scar. Blood drained from her face. Oh, no. She'd attacked him. The realization burned going down and sat like a rock at the base of her spine. The memory... She licked her dry lips, tried to swallow the tightness in her throat, and blinked to clear her head. "I'm sorry. I didn't mean—"

"You don't need to apologize to me for protecting yourself, Doc." His voice lowered an octave as he helped her to her feet. "Ever. Understand?"

She nodded but couldn't seem to let him go. "I remembered him."

Taking one hand in his, he rested her palm against his chest. The steady thump of his heart in her palm centered her, kept her from getting lost in the nightmares. The distinct line between his brows deeper, his eyes narrowing in on her. "Who?"

"The man who forced me to write that confession." She ran her free hand over her forehead, trying to release the pressure building in her head. Didn't help. She had a feeling nothing would help until whoever was doing this was caught. Her next words caught in her throat, no matter how many times she tried forcing them. "He killed her in front of me. He killed Alexis."

"You remember what he looks like?" he asked. "Recognize him?"

She shook her head, still fighting to slow her racing heart. "Not really. I think he was tall with blond hair. I feel like I should know him, though." She squeezed her eyes shut, but the pain only intensified. "He told me I'd never remember any of it, but I remember, Elliot. I saw the scar on the back of his hand. The skin looked burned."

"If his hand matches the rest of him, we'll have our suspect by the end of the day." His voice slid through her, all that sarcasm and confidence chasing back the fear clawing its way up her throat. "If it's a recent injury, within the last five years, my lab can help narrow the suspect pool by requesting medical records noted with that kind of injury."

She'd witnessed Alexis's murder, but she couldn't remember the most important parts of it. Taking a solid breath, she reveled in the feel of strength beneath Elliot's shirt, but pulled her hand away. He'd kissed her just outside this apartment, helped her forget. But it'd been a mistake. On both their parts. He wasn't interested in taking their friendship a step further, but in reality, there was no step further. Not for her. "I need to get my stuff. I'll meet you outside."

"You sure?" Suspicion narrowed his focus as she nodded, the weight of his attention pressurizing the air in her lungs. He hiked a thumb over his shoulder toward the front door. "In that case, I'll check in to see how deep my boss wants to bury me for not filling the team in sooner."

"Just give me a couple minutes." Waylynn waited until he closed the door behind him, then headed into her bedroom with uneasy steps. Not even the bright turquoise and yellow decorations could hide the fact her apartment had been used as a crime scene. Twenty-four hours ago her room had been filled with police searching for evidence, but Anchorage PD hadn't found the wall safe. She would've heard from her lawyer by now had that been the case.

Another flash of memory threatened to cement her feet in place as she glanced toward the closed bathroom door, but she kept moving. She couldn't stop. Couldn't think about what'd happened for fear she'd bolt out the front door. Turning her back on the epicenter of the crime scene, she hauled the print of Van Gogh's *Starry Night* off its nail to reveal the safe she'd installed when she'd moved in. The small LED light turned green at the scan of her fingerprint. Passport, fifty thousand in cash, personal documents. She pushed them to the side and went for the object she'd wrapped in an old T-shirt at the back first, its physical weight nothing compared with the heaviness compressing her chest. She stuffed the rest into her bag. Just in case, but she wasn't going anywhere until she uncovered who'd turned her world upside down.

Waylynn shut the wall safe and secured it before unearthing a weekend bag from her closet. Setting the gun at the bottom, she pulled clothing from hangers and shoved them inside. She changed out of the borrowed sweats from Officer Ramsey. She was a survivor. She always had been. Slinging the bag over one shoulder, she slipped into her most comfortable flats and closed the front door behind her for the last time.

This was the start of how it all ended.

And she sure as hell wasn't going down without a fight.

Chapter Six

"Well, this crisis came sooner than expected." Elliot hit the red button on his phone's screen to end the call. Five in the morning. The sun had gotten a little bit brighter in the east and the Blackhawk Security team was all over him. Over twenty-four hours since he'd found Waylynn in her bathroom, soaked in water and blood with a dead woman beside her. Now he'd gotten the news the hard drive they'd taken from Alexis Jacobs's apartment was encrypted. It would take their network security analyst, Elizabeth Dawson, over a day, maybe longer, to untangle the information the lab assistant had stored on the device. He'd witnessed the fear carved into Waylynn's expression when he'd found her doubled over in the hallway a few minutes ago. A fear that'd burned through his whole body. They were no closer to uncovering who'd put that fear in her eyes than they were twelve hours ago.

"What crisis?" That voice. *Her* voice. Soft, sexy, alluring enough to pull him deeper into uncharted and dangerous waters with a mere word. Every nerve ending he owned shot into awareness. Always had. Waylynn moved into his peripheral vision, a brightly colored tote bag slung over one shoulder. She'd changed her clothes. The black leggings, black sweatshirt and flat shoes were perfect for her slight curves. He appreciated the pragmatism. The view wasn't bad either. "I still hope we're friends after I taser you for looking at me like that."

A laugh rumbled through him. He never could slide one past her. "Get what you need?"

"Yes. Thank you. It's nice to have my own stuff." She smoothed her hand over the bag, the hollowness at her throat and shadowing her cheeks more apparent than a couple of hours ago. "Officer Ramsey's sweats were fine. They just weren't…mine. Having something familiar makes me feel a bit better about being a suspect in yet another murder. As does a toothbrush. So what's the crisis?"

Elliot redirected his attention from the hard-edged outline at the bottom of her bag. Right. The investigation. "The drive we recovered from your assistant's apartment is encrypted."

"What does that mean for the investigation?" Waylynn folded her arms, accentuating strong, lean muscle down her biceps. She'd hit the gym at Genism every morning as long as he'd known her, and it showed. She was the most determined woman he'd ever met, stubborn, infuriating, compassionate, and… His control had cracked a little when he'd kissed her.

He'd done it to prove there'd been nothing between them, that they could work together without his emotions getting in the way, but, hell, he'd certainly been wrong about that. The second he'd set his mouth against hers, the molten lava that'd been building beneath his skin had erupted to the surface and destroyed everything in its path. Including his reasons for avoiding committed relationships. It'd taken everything in him not to sweep her into his arms and take her back to his cabin. Make her forget the investigation, the fact she'd been framed for murder. He'd have helped her forget her name given the chance.

"Means we have time for you to get some beauty sleep and put something other than peanut-butter-frosted cookies in you." He headed down the stairs toward the parked SUV.

Space. He needed space. A few feet, a couple of minutes. Anything to clear her scent from his system and break the gravitational effect she seemed to have on him.

Her flats slapped against the cement stairs as she followed on his heels. "You'd be surprised how long I can live off chocolate and peanut butter."

"I have no doubt." Wrenching open the SUV's passenger door, Elliot motioned her inside. He rounded to the driver's side and climbed behind the wheel. Less than a minute later, he pulled out of the parking lot and a low ringing reached his ears.

She pulled the phone from her bag. "It's Dr. Stover again. Probably wondering when I'm coming back to work."

"Put it on speaker." The muscles in his neck ticked at the tension straining her voice. She'd been through hell the last two days. It'd take a lot more than thirty hours to get back some semblance of normal. Elliot headed south, back to the Seward Highway on-ramp.

She tapped the speaker button on the screen. "This is Dr. Hargraves."

"Waylynn, I'm glad you picked up. Listen, I know you've been through a lot the past couple days, but I couldn't stop them." Static reached through Matt Stover's end of the line. "I wanted to be the one to call to tell you the news myself."

"Stop who? What are you talking about?" The heaviness tinting Waylynn's question pressurized the air in Elliot's lungs. Three distinct lines deepened between her eyebrows. This wasn't good.

Elliot glanced down at her phone, the screen counting the length of the call. Nothing out of the ordinary. The timer came standard with that model, but the phone in Waylynn's hand didn't have her signature cracked screen in the top right-hand corner. One night after coming home from work, she'd dropped her phone on the stairs and damaged that corner. He'd caught her before she fell, but her phone hadn't been so lucky. That'd been six months ago.

She'd replaced either the screen or the phone recently. Why wait that long? "Is that a company phone?"

"Who's with you?" Dr. Stover asked.

"It's my frien—next-door neighbor. He was helping me get some of my things from my apartment." Waylynn swiped the stray hair coming out of her ponytail away from her face. "Matt, tell me what's going on."

"The board had an emergency meeting." The growl of a car engine overwhelmed Dr. Stover's voice. "In the wake of everything that's happened, you're being let go."

Elliot's attention snapped to her as they sped toward the highway. Oh, hell.

"On what grounds?" Waylynn shook her head, resting her elbow against the passenger side door. Her voice rose with each word out of her mouth. "Genism has profited off my research for ten years. They can't fire me."

It was five o'clock in the morning. Why would her boss—former boss—call Waylynn that early unless he knew she wasn't asleep? His instincts screamed warning as he wrenched the wheel to the left, turning them around. "Hang up the phone."

"What?" Those ocean-blue eyes widened with confusion. She planted her free hand against the dashboard to keep her balance as they turned back the way they'd come. "What's wrong?"

"Waylynn?" Matt Stover asked. "What's going on?"

Elliot grabbed for the phone and tossed it out the window.

Waylynn spun in her seat to track the phone's landing out the back window. "What are you doing?"

"Your assistant broke corporate policy to store company information on that drive we recovered. Which means whoever killed her had to have known she'd taken it in the first place." Elliot pressed the accelerator to the floor, glancing into the rearview mirror for a tail. Damn it, he should've noticed the phone before now.

"Okay, so it had to be someone in Genism. That doesn't explain why you threw my phone out the window." Her voice hollowed as she straightened in her seat. "I got a new phone a few weeks ago after Matt noticed I'd broken the screen on the last one."

"I knew I never liked that guy." Elliot shook his head, knuckles white on the steering wheel. "The bastard has been tracking you through your company phone. Probably listening to all of your conversations."

"Matt wouldn't do that. We've worked together for years. We're friends," she said. "Where're we going? Your cabin is in the other direction."

"Blackhawk Security." The light turned green up ahead and he pushed the SUV harder. Downtown Anchorage passed in a rush out the side windows. Theories as to why Genism would be tracking Waylynn crossed his mind, but he couldn't think about that right now. He forced himself to focus. Get her to safety. Then track down the SOB who'd dared come after her. "You're officially in protective custody." He used the controls on the steering wheel to call the team.

"I just got off the phone with you." Blackhawk's founder and CEO's voice filled the interior of the car. Sullivan Bishop didn't wait for an answer. "Please tell me you haven't already dug yourself a deeper—"

"Mango." His boss would know what the code word meant. Elliot checked the rearview mirror again. No movement.

"ETA?" The former SEAL's tone dipped into dangerous territory. Sullivan had formed the team to protect those whom the police and other law enforcement agencies couldn't or wouldn't bother with. Waylynn Hargraves qualified. His boss—and the entire Blackhawk Security team—would do what was necessary to keep her safe.

"Two minutes." He studied Waylynn. The tension tightening her grip on the edge of the seat was enough to lock his jaw. He should've noticed her phone earlier. They could've gotten ahead of this thing for once. "One civilian."

"We're ready." Sullivan ended the call, but Elliot couldn't relax yet.

The front of the SUV crossed into the intersection. Two more minutes and she'd be safe. She'd—

Headlights brightened through his window a split second before the crash. Rubber on asphalt screeched in his ears as Waylynn's side of the vehicle slammed into the light post. Glass shattered around them, metal screaming against metal.

Momentum rocked Elliot sideways in his seat, smashing his head against the window as air bags deployed. The smell of burned rubber and gasoline filled his system. Son of a bitch. He hadn't seen that coming. A wave of dizziness and pain darkened the edges of his vision and he rubbed the base of his palm into his eye. One breath. Two. Headlights from the vehicle that'd T-boned them flickered. Copper and salt filled his mouth. Blood. He squinted away from the blinding light, searching for her in the passenger seat among the air bags in his way. She'd been wearing a seat belt, right? He couldn't remember, the pounding at the crown of his head overwhelming. Reaching out, he brushed his hand against her arm as glass crunched outside the vehicle. Footsteps. Elliot disengaged his seat belt, his vision clearing in slow increments. "Waylynn."

She didn't answer. Didn't move.

"Waylynn." He pushed every ounce of energy he had into her name. Dread curdled in his gut. He slid his hand along the side of her face and turned her toward him. Planting his fingers at her throat, he exhaled hard in relief. Strong pulse. She was alive. There was no way they'd be able to get out of the SUV through either of the doors with what looked like another SUV on his side and the streetlamp on hers. Elliot compressed the button to her seat belt. They'd have to go out the back. He shook his head to clear the high-pitched keen ringing in his ears. The mission hadn't changed, only the circumstances: get her to safety. "Come on, Doc. We gotta get out of here."

He climbed over the seat into the back row, his boots sliding against broken glass on the floor, and pulled a lockbox from under the hidden compartment beneath the floor mat. Thumbing in the combination, Elliot pocketed the gun's extra magazine and ammunition and tucked the small handgun down the waistband of his jeans at the small of his back. No sirens. Blackhawk Security SUVs came loaded with trackers. The team would find the vehicle in the next few minutes, but his instincts said they didn't have that long. Genism had been tracking Waylynn for weeks. No telling whom they'd sent after her, but a company with that many resources and that much power wouldn't hire an amateur. He leveraged his weight into the back of the seats and kicked the rear window as hard as he could. The bulletproof glass dislodged in one piece, crashing to the ground.

Movement registered off to his right, beyond the vehicle that'd smashed into them. The driver? Had they made it out okay? Rough breathing reached his ears over the shuffling of broken glass. "Help." The man's voice rocketed Elliot's blood pressure higher. "I need help!"

"Hang on, buddy. I'm coming." Elliot didn't hesitate. He climbed from the back of the SUV, but an earth-shattering wave of pain from the crash shot down his spine and unbalanced him. He landed on top of the bulletproof glass, a groan working up his throat. He was going to feel that in a couple of hours. His head pounded loud behind his ears, but the ringing had stopped. "I'm okay."

The streetlamp reflected off a classic pair of dark oxford shoes as he rolled to his side. Two Taser nodes latched on to his shirt, but before he could reach for them twelve hundred volts of electricity shot through him at the push of a button. Fire burned his nerves and muscles. Elliot rolled onto his back, unable to control his movements. His jaw clenched hard, his entire body rigid from the current. The headache at the back of his skull exploded in a haze of white light. A growl ripped from his throat. Waylynn. He had to get to Waylynn.

The current faded, but his peripheral nervous system had yet to get the message. Elliot struggled to keep his eyes open, to reach for his gun. To do anything but lie there, leaving Waylynn vulnerable. "Don't…touch her."

The masked assailant who'd tasered him crouched low, retrieving the Taser's electrodes one by one. "Try to stop me."

SHE GASPED INTO consciousness as a high-voltage shock wave of fear slid down her spine. Pain exploded from the right side of her head. They'd… They'd been in an accident. They'd been hit. Waylynn fought to raise her head, but the darkness, the fatigue, tempted her to close her eyes again. Go to sleep. No. She had to stay awake. Dim lighting glinted off the broken glass in her lap. She set her head back against the headrest and scanned the rest of the vehicle. "Elliot?"

His name clawed from her dry throat as she searched the empty interior. She swallowed against the bile rising up her throat. Oh, no. The driver's side window had been shattered. Had he been thrown from the SUV? Panic overwhelmed her as she reached to unlatch her seat belt, but found the buckle already unlocked. She was sure she'd buckled herself when she'd gotten in the car. Had to be Elliot. Where was he? Her muscles protested as she climbed across the center console. Ignoring the slice of glass in her palms, she rested her weight against his still-warm seat. Distant sirens reached her ears. The police were on their way. "Answer me, Elliot."

"Sorry, Dr. Hargraves, your bodyguard won't be answering anything for a while." Gloved hands shot through the driver's side window and pulled her from the SUV.

"Wait, I have to find my friend. He was in the vehicle with me. He could be hurt." Waylynn struggled against his vise-like grip, unwilling to leave the scene until she recovered Elliot. No. She wasn't going to the hospital. Not without him, but the man pulling her from the crash was too strong. So much bigger than her and her injuries had taken a lot of her strength. The scene of the crash blurred as he set her on her feet and spun her to face him. Her head throbbed in rhythm to her racing pulse as the dizziness cleared. The black ski mask hiding his features plunged dread straight through her. What kind of emergency personnel wore a mask? The hardness in his impossibly black eyes and his hold still wrapped around her wrists told her the answer. They didn't.

His six-foot-plus frame towered over her. Black ski mask, dark jacket, black pants, black shoes. Gloves. "He'll be fine once he wakes up."

He'd called her Dr. Hargraves. She'd never told him her name.

"Let me go." She pulled at her wrists locked between his hands, the scent of cigarettes burning her nose. This wasn't the man from her quick flash of memory back at her apartment. He'd had blue eyes, but fear skittered through her all the same. She glanced at the smoking vehicle that'd T-boned them in the intersection, the driver's-side door propped open. No driver to be seen. Because he was standing in front of her. Waylynn swept her tongue through the saltiness in her mouth. "You caused the crash?"

"You should've taken the fall for Alexis's murder, Waylynn." Her masked assailant pulled her into him, repositioning one hand around her throat. "Would've made this so much easier. Shame, too. I think your work could've changed the world."

Could've?

His hand shot to her throat, cutting off her oxygen. Waylynn tried to pry his grip from her, but he pulled a gun from the waistband of his pants and lodged it into her rib cage. Black cobwebs snaked into the edges of her vision. "P-please—"

"Why don't you point that thing at someone your own size?" That voice.

A combination of recognition and hesitation slid through her. She'd know that voice anywhere, but right now, it sounded…different. Waylynn searched the wreckage through the holes that hadn't darkened in her vision, jerking in her captor's hold. Movement registered from the back of the totaled SUV, urging her to step back, but her abductor kept a tight grip. Shadows retreated from his face as Elliot moved beneath the pool of light from the streetlamp. A gasp caught in her throat. Blood chilled in her veins, yet beads of sweat slid from her temples. He was alive. Goose bumps prickled across the small of her back. He was…not the Elliot she knew.

No. The shadow standing ten feet from her had turned into something far more threatening. Waylynn pulled at her attacker's wrist, her body screaming for air. Pressure built in her lungs. A single second stretched into hours, the darkness closing in faster.

"I'll have to use a higher voltage on you next time." Her abductor's hand loosened enough for her to gulp down a lungful of oxygen as he took aim at her best friend.

Warning trickled down her spine.

"There won't be a next time." A predatory growl escaped from Elliot's mouth, raising the hairs on the back of her neck. Violence stared out through the gray eyes she'd dreamed about for months. A shadow of that same violence darkened his expression. "Now get your damn hands off her."

Elliot didn't wait for an answer and rushed forward.

She wanted to scream. Couldn't with the hand around her neck. The explosion of gunfire rocked through her. Her ears rang as his shoulder ripped back from catching the bullet. His guttural groan ignited the burn of desperation. Waylynn tried to lunge forward to catch him before he hit the ground but was pulled back into her attacker. She launched her elbow into a wall of muscle, only her captor's exhale an indication she'd done any damage. That small amount of vulnerability pushed her harder.

Elliot had collapsed to one knee, his knuckles against asphalt, eyes shut tight.

Slamming her heel into the top of her assailant's foot, she got him to release her. She twisted out of his reach, gulped as much air as she could, and rocketed the base of her palm into where she thought his nose might be under the mask. "Get off of me!"

The satisfying crunch of bone reached her ears. She raced to take control of the gun in his hand, but she wasn't fast enough. A strong backhand across her face knocked her to the ground. Stinging pain lanced through her head as she fell, the city street nothing but a blur.

"You shouldn't have done that." Elliot's swing

unbalanced the gunman, but another squeeze of the trigger arced a bullet wide over Waylynn's head. They had to get out of here. "Waylynn, run!"

She covered her head in a vain attempt to stop the bullet with her hands. The sirens she'd heard earlier seemed to fade. Where were the police? Why wasn't anybody helping? Blood dripped from Elliot's shoulder. His movements were slowing. He wouldn't last much longer without help. Shoving to her feet, she searched the scene for something—anything—he could use as a weapon.

The crunch of glass against asphalt followed by a rough groan from over her shoulder forced her to turn back to the fight. Her attacker had pinned Elliot against the colliding vehicle and raised the gun once more. Another hit to the face twisted his head in one direction. The second hit wrenched his head again. "Stop! You're going to kill him!"

Her attacker punched Elliot over and over, those dark gray eyes locked on her.

"No!" Waylynn pumped her legs hard, then latched on to the masked man's arm to give Elliot a fighting chance. But a solid kick to the midsection sent her flying back. She couldn't breathe. Couldn't think. Only adrenaline kept her moving. There. Waylynn crawled toward a piece of the damaged streetlamp, loose gravel digging into her knees. Sliding her fingers around the metal, she pushed to her feet and hiked the steel above her shoulder on unsteady legs. "Get the hell away from him. Now."

"Waylynn...run." Blood trickled down Elliot's bottom lip as he swayed on his feet, the skin swollen and cracked.

Waylynn fought off the paralysis threatening to overwhelm her. She'd never attacked another human being before. Never wanted to hurt someone as much as she wanted to hurt the man with the gun right now. "I said back away."

She adjusted her grip around the pipe and swiped her tongue across her increasingly dry lips. Her gut clenched as Elliot slid down the side of the vehicle, his normally bright gaze clouded. He was losing blood too fast. She had to get him to the hospital.

"You should've listened to your bodyguard, Dr. Hargraves. You should've run while you had the chance." A low rumble of a laugh filled her ears, dread pooling at the base of her spine. No matter what happened in the next few minutes, she'd remember that laugh for the rest of her life. Something pure and evil crawled over her skin. That black gaze forced ice through her veins. "Those sirens you heard? A distraction of mine. Anchorage PD won't have enough patrols to answer this call. Nobody is coming to save you."

She glanced at Elliot losing consciousness at her feet. The bullet could still be inside him, could be causing permanent damage. Not to mention the other dozen injuries he'd incurred since the crash. They were running out of time. Elliot would die right here in the middle of the street if she didn't do something.

He'd protected her this far. Now it was her turn to return the favor. "I don't need anyone to save me."

Waylynn swung the pipe as hard as she could.

Her attacker caught it midswing and wrenched the steel from her hand. She didn't hesitate, lashing out at him with her opposite hand, but the strike did nothing. She didn't work for Blackhawk Security. She hadn't been trained in hand-to-hand combat or joined the military. She was a scientist, a researcher. She spent most of her days glued to the computer screen analyzing genetic samples under her microscope.

But she wouldn't let him take her and she wasn't going to let Elliot die.

The clang of metal on asphalt rang loud in her ears as he tossed her makeshift weapon and advanced. She stumbled back, the heel of her flats catching on chunks of loose debris from the crash. No. Waylynn fisted her hands, taking a stand. "His team is already on the way."

"They can't help you now, Dr. Hargraves. You brought your bodyguard into this mess, and he'll die because of you." Her attacker raised the gun, taking aim at her head. "Then it'll be your turn."

Chapter Seven

"Over here!" an unfamiliar voice called.

A bright light passed over him, footsteps and shouts close enough to pull Elliot from unconsciousness. Pain shot across his shoulder and down his arm. His head throbbed at the base of his skull.

"Tell me he's not dead." Now, that voice he recognized. Sullivan.

Cold fingers slid across his neck and he hissed in reaction. "Pulse is weak, but he's alive. He's lost a lot of blood."

Different voice.

"You say the nicest things, Kate." He struggled to see the psychologist's face. Squinting against the circle of flashlights around him, Elliot moved to lift his arm to block the light but couldn't. Right. A bullet tended to have that effect. He ran his tongue along the split inside his cheek, then leaned over and spit blood. Digging his heels into the ground, he pressed his back against the vehicle behind him and pushed to his feet slowly to face the team. Oh, hell. He felt like he'd been hit by a train. Or at least a Mack truck. Pieces of memory bled into place. They'd been attacked. The son of a bitch had gone after Waylynn right before he'd lost consciousness. "Where is she? Where's Waylynn?"

"You tell us." Sullivan Bishop centered himself in his vision as Kate Monroe, Blackhawk Security's profiler, moved out of the way. Vincent, Glennon, Anthony, Elizabeth. Even Elizabeth's baby daddy, Braxton, stood around him. The gang was all there. "What happened?"

"Bastard plowed into us. Tasered me to get to her. I fought him off, but he put a bullet in my shoulder. Lost too much blood." The haze cleared with every inhale. He was still losing blood. Then he spotted the piece of pipe she'd threatened to bash her attacker with in the middle of the street. Rage diluted the pain and spread like wildfire. Her abductor wanted a battle? If the son of a bitch damaged a single hair on her head, Elliot would bring a war. He shoved through the semicircle his team had built around him. "Get out of my way."

They couldn't have gotten far. Everything about this investigation—the death of Waylynn's assistant, the destruction of her research, the recovered hard drive, the tracking device in her phone—it all tied back to Genism Corporation. He'd never met Dr. Matthew Stover, but it stood to reason he was the one who'd been tracking her since giving her the phone a few weeks ago.

Anthony Harris, the team's weapons expert, barricaded himself, arms folded, in front of Elliot's escape route. "I've seen that look, man. Hell, I've given that look to everyone who came between me and Glennon. You've lost a lot of blood. Tell me what you need, and I'll recover her while you get patched up."

His reflection stared back at him from Anthony's damn aviator sunglasses. Blood dripped down his face, his lip busted. Not to mention the injuries he couldn't see. The bullet in his shoulder, the possible cracked rib he'd taken to give Waylynn a chance to run. He'd failed her once. It took every ounce of energy he had to keep standing, but he wouldn't fail her again. He'd take a hundred more bullets if it meant keeping her safe. Rolling his shoulder forward, he clenched his teeth against the pain screaming through his arm. The bullet was still inside, tearing through muscle and tendon, but every second that bastard had Waylynn led to a higher chance he wouldn't be able to find her. And that wasn't an option. He wouldn't lose her. Not now. Not ever. Elliot stretched out his hand. "Keys."

"Take mine. None of you have wrecked it yet. Want backup?" Kate didn't hesitate, a half smile curling at one edge of her pale mouth as she tossed the keys. He shook his head. This was something he had to do on his own. The psychologist-turned-profiler folded her arms. Medium-length, platinum blonde hair framed a thin face and wide green eyes. At five foot ten, Kate Monroe demanded attention with a single look, but the shroud of grief from losing her husband to a former patient last year kept most people at a distance. But Elliot knew the truth. Of all of the men and women on this team, Kate was the biggest softy of them all. She nodded. "You've been shot, beaten and we found you unconscious."

"I'm fine." Nothing would stop him from getting to Waylynn.

"Try not to get yourself shot again," Vincent said. "Or killed."

Elliot curled his hand around the keys, then circled around Anthony without looking back at the rest of his team. He wouldn't need backup. Didn't need a weapon. He'd tear the son of bitch who dared take Waylynn from him with his bare hands.

A thin veil of snow dusted the ground as he rounded to the driver's side of Kate's SUV and climbed in. What kind of hell city snowed in the middle of June? The engine growled to life at the turn of a key, the entire team staring at him through the windshield as he spun away from the scene.

Red and blue police cruiser lights flashed across his vision as he programmed Genism's address into the vehicle's navigation system. Sullivan and Anthony would stall Anchorage PD as long as they could. Elliot had more important things to worry about. There was only one place this could end, one place he bet the man who'd framed Waylynn for murder would take her.

"I'm coming for you, Doc." Headlights reflected

off wet road, but Elliot only pressed the accelerator harder. He squeezed his knuckles around the steering wheel, the scrapes and cuts along the back of his hands still bleeding. Whoever had come after her wasn't some geneticist. He'd never known a lab researcher to fight like that. He swiped at the blood running down his mouth. No, the son of a bitch who'd taken Waylynn was something more. Former military, maybe a trained federal operative. But that didn't explain the connection to his next-door neighbor or her employer. Unless Genism Corporation had hired someone to come after her on their behalf.

Didn't matter right now. Getting Waylynn back, having her in his arms again, that was all that mattered. They'd deal with the rest once he recovered her. Together. The slight sigh that'd escaped from her as he'd kissed her replayed in his head. Blistering-hot blood rushed through his system. He'd get her back. He had to. "You better be alive."

Tires screeched on pavement as he fishtailed the SUV into Genism Corporation's main parking lot. Streetlamps flickered, then died, the sun peeking out from behind the Chugach Mountain Range. No sign of another vehicle. Nothing to indicate her abductor had brought her here. His gut said he was in the right place. Stretching his arm into the back seat, Elliot suppressed a scream working up his throat as he reached for the lockbox under the bench seat. A faint pop registered beneath muscle and he exhaled hard through the pain. Damn bullet wouldn't stop him from finding her.

Nothing would.

Slamming a fresh magazine into his spare Glock, he loaded a round and checked the safety. His boots hit the ground, the hairs on the back of his neck standing on end. As though he'd been centered in someone else's crosshairs. He scanned the lab's rooftop—still nothing—then headed for the main doors. Warning exploded through him, but what was life without a little risk? Elliot tightened his grip around the gun. He wrenched the glass door handle and raised the gun, pushing his way inside the stark white lobby.

Silence. No cars in the parking lot, no security on location. Yet the lab's front door had been left unlocked. "That doesn't seem very responsible."

A pair of black shoes sticking out from behind the large receptionist desk pulled him forward. Checking over this shoulder, Elliot crouched beside a female guard who'd been relieved of the weapon that was supposed to be in her holster. A line of blood trickled onto her cheekbone, but the rise and fall of her chest indicated she'd only been knocked unconscious. He pulled his phone from his pocket and requested an ambulance to the lab. Scuff marks veered off to the left, stark black against the white tile leading deeper into the lab. Caused by Waylynn's shoes as her abductor dragged her down the hall? Shoving to his feet, he hefted the gun to shoulder level. Pain exploded down his arm, but it wouldn't slow him down. Anchorage PD was about to have their hands full with another body on this case.

A high-pitched scream echoed down the hallway, an all-too-familiar sound that jacked his blood pressure higher.

"Waylynn." Every cell in his body caught fire as he followed the sound. White walls and tile blurred in his vision, his gut tight. Clear glass windows and expensive equipment was all he could see as he passed lab after lab. He'd heard her—she'd been close—but there were too many rooms in this damn facility to know where the SOB had taken her. Elliot slowed. Focused. His lungs worked overtime, but he forced himself to listen harder. She was here. She was alive. He was close.

"You don't have to do this." Her voice shook and Elliot slowed. The scent of geraniums filled his lungs and he breathed her in deeper as he pressed himself back against the nearest wall for cover. Waylynn. "Nobody else has to get hurt. Please."

The static sound of tape coming off the roll filled the silence. Elliot chanced a glance around the corner. There, in the center of the room, Waylynn had been duct taped at the wrists and ankles to a black office chair. Right in front of her stood the bastard who'd taken her with another piece of tape stretched between his hands. Her abductor leaned forward to secure the strip over her mouth. She struggled to free herself from the grip at the back of her neck and Elliot tightened his hand around the Glock. The SOB had hit her once. He wouldn't touch her again. Elliot swung gun-first into the lab, the scent of chemicals strong in the air. "Looks like I'm late to the party."

Only the man's dark eyes were visible through the black ski mask, the shooter's hands raised in surrender. One wrong move. That was all it would take to give Elliot a reason to pull the trigger.

"That was easy." The gun wavered in his hand as he closed in on the suspect. "What? You're not going to shoot me again? How about another round of electricity?"

Waylynn struggled to speak through the tape, but only mumbled sounds reached his ears. Warning flared in her gaze.

Fluorescent lighting reflected back off some kind of liquid on the floor. The chemical smell. Elliot caught sight of the empty bottle on the desk beside Waylynn—isopropyl alcohol—and the lighter in the shooter's hand. "Oh, hell."

THEY WERE DEAD.

Relief at seeing Elliot alive warred with the suffocating panic clawing up her throat. If her kidnapper let go of that lighter, everyone in this room would burn. And there wouldn't be a thing she could do about it. Waylynn pulled at the tape securing her to the chair. One edge slipped off the hem of her sweatshirt and her pulse jerked a bit higher. Could she get to the kidnapper before he killed them all?

She twisted her wrists again, attention on her attacker. She'd almost lost her best friend once. She couldn't do it again, couldn't watch him die in front of her. Although the entire bottle of alcohol her abductor had emptied onto the floor around her might solve that problem faster than she wanted.

"Drop that lighter and I'll make you wish you'd killed me when you had the chance." Blood stained Elliot's jacket and jeans. Awareness flooded through her as he flinched against the pain he must've felt from the bullet.

"You couldn't stop me after the crash. You can't stop me now, Dunham." He knew Elliot's name? Of course he did. He knew everything about them it seemed. Her name, where she worked, knew Elliot. A sharp hiss escaped the lighter as the attacker who'd run them off the road ignited the flame. No. No, no, no, no. This wasn't happening. "Dr. Hargraves isn't walking out of this building alive. Nothing personal."

It sure seemed personal to her.

Her kidnapper dropped the lighter.

"No!" Elliot launched forward.

She screamed through the tape as her captor bolted for the lab's side door. Flames ignited all around her, the heat instantly too much to take. Fists clenched, she pulled at the tape around her wrists, but where there'd been leeway before, she couldn't break the binding. Elliot pulled up short outside the ring of flames. Her heart threatened to beat out of her chest. He couldn't get through. Couldn't get to her without getting burned. Black smoke climbed toward the ceiling as one of the nearby desks caught fire. The sprinklers would put out the flames before they reached her. Everything would be okay.

"Waylynn!" Elliot holstered his weapon, then covered his face as the fire lashed out at him.

She wedged her toes against the floor and tried to push away from the flames. In vain. Her abductor had sandwiched her between a lab desk and the ring of fire. There was no way out. Why hadn't the emergency system responded? No alarms. No sprinklers. A sob broke through the panic and she closed her eyes. No. She couldn't die like this. Blue-based flames inched their way toward her as the linoleum beneath the alcohol melted from the heat.

"Hang on, Doc." Elliot covered his mouth and backed up a few feet. "I'll get you out of here."

He was going to jump through the fire to try to save her. He'd burn right in front of her and there was nothing she could do to help him. No. He needed to get out of here. Needed to go after the shooter who'd put a bullet in his shoulder. Waylynn shook her head, pressing herself back into the chair. She flexed her jaw, worked at the tape around her mouth. Heated air burned down her esophagus and she couldn't yell for him to stop. An acrid smell dived deep into her lungs as the edge of the office chair singed. Sweat beaded along her hairline and at the nape of her neck. Her feet had been taped too high off the ground. She couldn't move. She shook her head again.

Elliot jumped.

The tape kept her scream at bay. Blood rushed to her head, too fast, too hard. The small amount of air she'd been holding pressurized in her lungs, but faster than she thought possible, rough hands were tugging at her wrists. She pulled at the duct tape again, trying to get it off as fast as possible.

"I always thought you were smoking hot, but this is a bit much, don't you think?" Elliot cut the tape from her wrists with a small blade in his hand, then crouched in front of her to get to her ankles.

She doubled over to work at the other side, then pulled the tape from her mouth. Standing, she shoved him. "What were you thinking? You could've died, and I wouldn't have been able to do anything."

He slid an arm around her waist and pulled her into him. The flames threatening to consume the entire lab—chemicals and everything—were nothing compared with the heat in his eyes at that moment. "I protect what's mine."

Waylynn sucked down a lungful of tainted oxygen. His? The growing heat around them battled with the tingling at the base of her spine. There was nowhere to go. The fire had spread too fast, but he'd protect her. She fisted his jacket, holding on to him with everything she had. "We're trapped."

"Climb up on the desk." Calluses scraped against her oversensitized skin as Elliot helped her onto the office chair she'd been bound to, then onto the desk. He followed after her, shedding his jacket in the process. Blood had spread across his white T-shirt, but he didn't seem to notice. "The smoke is getting thicker. Cover your mouth with this and follow my lead."

Dried blood flaked against her fingers as she held the jacket up to her face. Her eyes stung, smoke filling every square inch of the room. Where were they supposed to go? The exits had been blocked by the flames. More sections of the floor were melting. Fire ate oxygen. They'd suffocate from smoke inhalation if they didn't get out of here soon. Waylynn clung to the wall of muscle somehow keeping her calm in the middle of a burning building.

Elliot spun her into him, the whites of his eyes reddening. Sweat dripped down into his beard. "Do you trust me?"

Trust him? He'd saved her life twice in the span of twenty-four hours. He was the only person in this world she could count on, the only man she'd let close. The only man she'd considered a friend. She nodded. "Yes."

"Then I need you to get up into the vent above us." Elliot crouched on top of the desk, then gazed up at her. "I'll give you a boost. Get as far from the fire as you can, get in the SUV and call my team."

Waylynn craned her neck to spot the vent through the thickening smoke. Okay. She could make it to the opening with a boost. Locking her gaze on him, she dropped the jacket beside her. She placed one foot in his cupped palms and latched on to him. Tiles fell from the ceiling a few feet away and she turned away from the embers flying through the air, nearly losing her balance. Strong arms pulled her back into him. Heat blistered along her back, the fire getting closer every second they wasted talking, but his words finally registered. *She* would get as far from the fire as she could. *She* would get to the SUV. *She* would call his team. "What about you? How will you get up?"

"I'll be right behind you." He glanced up at the vent again. "Come on. This desk isn't going to hold both of us for much longer."

But Waylynn didn't move. "For a recovering con man, you're not very good at lying."

"Maybe you're just the one person who can see through me." His hands feathered over her arms, only a hint of his clean, masculine scent surviving the hotter-than-hell temperatures. Putting his life in danger with the moose, taking a bullet for her back at the crash scene, now this. Elliot intertwined his fingers through hers and brought her palm to his mouth. His beard bristled along the skin there and a different kind of warmth trickled down her spine despite the encroaching flames. He closed his eyes for a split second and an understanding passed between them. He'd told her before: he'd do anything to keep her safe. Without warning, he crouched, wrapped his arms around her legs and hefted her above him.

"Elliot, no!" She pushed off the ceiling with one hand, clinging to him for balance with the other. "I'm not leaving you. I can't do this without you."

"Yes, you can, Waylynn." A groan escaped up his throat as he pushed her higher with his injured shoulder. He never called her Waylynn. Which meant... "Get in and don't look back. Do not come back for me."

No. She pulled at the metal seam of the vent, flinching as the crash of steel on wood reverberated through her ears. Scrambling straight up into the duct, she exhaled hard at the burn of metal against her skin. Pitch-black darkness greeted her on either side. With some maneuvering, she leveraged one hand on the edge of the opening and reached back through to him. "Grab my hand. I can pull you up."

"Get out of here, Doc. That vent can't support us both." Elliot protected his face as one corner of the desk they'd stood on together caught fire. They were running out of time. Any minute now, their island of safety would burn right out from underneath him. He gathered the jacket from the table and covered his mouth and nose. "I'll find another way out."

"There is no other way out. Elliot, grab my hand!" She'd thought she'd lost him once. She couldn't do it again. Screw the investigation. Screw being framed for murder. Screw her research. Elliot Dunham was the only person in this world who mattered, the only person who was more important than breathing. More important than food or water or her apartment. He'd risk all that? Smoke dived deep into her lungs, burned her eyes, and she moved to cover her mouth with her arm. She couldn't last up here much longer. The smoke was pooling inside the vent system, but she wouldn't leave him behind. Never. "How are you supposed to protect me if you're dead?"

"I've survived this long, haven't I? Get out of the building, Waylynn. I'll find you." He shifted closer to one edge of the desk without looking up at her.

And jumped.

Aluminum cut into her palms as she gripped the vent opening. "Elliot!"

Chapter Eight

Son of a bitch. When would people stop trying to set him on fire?

Waylynn's scream died as the fire roared loud in his ears and he hoped like hell she was getting as far from this building as possible. He would've climbed into that vent right after her if he'd believed the airshaft would take both of their weight. Alas, that was not the case.

A rafter splintered above him, cracks in the exposed wood a bright, glowing orange. He'd run out of time. The isopropyl alcohol Waylynn's abductor had emptied onto the floor wasn't the only chemical the lab kept on hand. This entire building was a Molotov cocktail waiting to explode. "Right. Exit plan."

Going out the window wasn't an option. The bookcases, desks and chairs had already been consumed by the flames. Another foot toward the flames was too much for his exposed skin to take. Elliot squinted into the brightening fury closing in on him. Smoke clouded his airway and he jumped to the floor. Memories of a downtown apartment, a stalker, a crowbar to the head and Sullivan Bishop throwing him over his shoulder rushed to the front of his mind. He and his boss had been working Jane Reise's case a few months ago and the suspect they'd been tracking hadn't been too happy about their coming into his personal space. Well, at least no one had knocked him unconscious this time. If he played his cards right, he could make it through the small line of tile that hadn't been affected by the fire yet. "I'm going to regret this."

He protected his face and ran straight to the nearest door through the narrow untouched space. Testing the handle with his jacket around his hand, he slammed his uninjured shoulder into the thick steel. The damn thing wouldn't budge. The lab's biohazard procedures must've locked down the entire room. But then why hadn't the sprinklers come on? He rammed his shoulder into the door one more time, a heavy thud barely registering over the crackling of fire. The bastard who'd started the fire must've turned them off. The room would've gone into quarantine at the sign of a fire or biohazard leak, but the sprinklers and other precautionary measures were useless now. Elliot spun to go back the way he'd come, but the clear path that'd been there a minute ago was gone. "Huh. Mom was right. I really am going to burn in hell."

Well, then at least he'd have the chance to see her

again. A burst of nervous laughter escaped but died as the seriousness of the situation took hold. He was going to die in this room. His family could take care of themselves. They always had. His team might mourn him, but they'd move on. But Waylynn? She didn't have anyone else. No family. No friends other than her colleagues and her work to keep her company. Even that had been destroyed. Elliot curled his fingers into his palms. He'd spent the last year telling himself nothing could happen between them after everything he'd been through, that his freedom, his happiness, took priority.

But, hell, Waylynn made him happy.

That smile when she spotted him with a beer when she came home after a long day of work, the fact humming "Gangsta's Paradise" brought out her infectious laugh every time, her determination to move on with her life despite her past. Everything about her made him want to be the man she deserved, made him want to be more than a con man. More than a private investigator. More than a friend.

Sweat slid down his face beneath his T-shirt. No. This wasn't how he was going out. Elliot reached for the gun in his shoulder. He'd shoot his way out if he had to. But came up empty. He searched the floor, spotting his gun a few feet from the desk he and Waylynn had used for a brief moment of safety. No way he could get to it now. New plan. Wrapping his jacket around his arm, he hiked his elbow into the pane of glass in the door. Two times. Three. He pushed the last remnants of his draining energy into the next three strikes, but the glass didn't so much as crack. The glass was meant to withstand an explosion in the lab, sealed to keep toxins in, in case of a bio-hazard lockdown. He wasn't getting through it without something heavier. He stepped back. He needed a microscope, a chair—anything—to punch through.

Without warning, the butt of a fire extinguisher crashed through the glass. Shards fell from the frame onto the floor. Those ocean-blue eyes settled on him. Ash streaked Waylynn's face, darkened the bruise across her cheek. Pieces of her long blond hair had singed ends. "You are not getting away from me that easily."

"What are you doing here?" A blend of fury and admiration flooded through him. He didn't know whether he wanted to kiss her or hike her over his shoulder and run for putting herself back in harm's way. Black smoke broke free through the broken glass. Escape first. Decide later. "I told you to get as far from this building as possible."

"I'm saving your life." She set the fire extinguisher on the floor and reached through the opening for him, fisting his T-shirt with skinned and bloody fingers. "But, sure, let's take the time we don't have to argue about it some more."

"Fine." Elliot hiked one leg through the broken windowpane, then fell onto the tile on the other side of the door. He couldn't suppress the groan working up his throat as pain spread through his shoulder and down his spine. His lungs spasmed with the rush of clean oxygen. He closed his eyes to relieve the sting, but they weren't out of the woods yet. The fire would spread to this room—and every room—now that Waylynn had shattered the window. They had to get out of there. And find the bastard who'd tried to kill them. "Tasered. Shot. Nearly burned alive. What else could go wrong today?"

"Elliot." His name on her lips—almost breath-like—raised his awareness of her to all all-time high. Something was wrong.

Elliot cracked his eyes. His shoulder protested as he hiked himself to his feet, but pain was nothing compared with the fire burning through his veins at the sight of that masked SOB pointing a gun to Waylynn's head. "Speak of the devil and he shall appear."

"Move and she's dead, Mr. Dunham," the arsonist said.

Waylynn flinched as her captor's grip on the tendon between her neck and shoulder visibly tightened.

"I don't think you want her dead. Otherwise you would've killed her already. You had opportunity. Motive is still a mystery, though." He might not be able to read the bastard's expression through that damn mask, but Elliot had already started putting the pieces together. Reading people was what he did. Everything he needed to know about a person was in their routine, in their actions. In the choices they made. All he had to do was solve the puzzle. It was how he'd conned so many people out of their money until a few years ago. And how he'd ended up in an Iraqi prison. "You started by framing her for murder, but when she hired a private investigator to clear her name, you destroyed her research, hoping that would bruise her enough to stop looking deeper. It didn't work so you had to try kidnapping, and the arson gave her enough time to get free. Even now, I can tell the safety on your gun is on. Either you don't want Waylynn dead or you're the worst killer I've ever seen."

The arsonist's gloved hand twitched alongside the gun as he shifted his weight between his feet. One second. Two. He turned the gun on Elliot and clicked off the safety. "You think you have me figured out, but I've done my research, too, Mr. Dunham. I know everything there is to know about you. How many people you've hurt, how much money you've stolen, where your family lives."

"You don't know anything about me if you think a threat like that is going to make me react." If anything, it was the shooter's hold on Waylynn that heated his blood now. That, and the fire threatening to kill them all. He glanced at her, at the slight movement she made with her eyes to the right. Without making it obvious, Elliot spotted the fire extinguisher beside him. Wouldn't survive against another bullet, but it was better than nothing. He nodded enough for her to notice.

"Put down the gun and let Waylynn go or I'm going to make you bleed. You don't want her dead, which means you need her for something." Sweat built down his spine as flames licked up the sides of the opening at his back. Shock slammed into him with the force of a knife to the gut. "Or you know her."

Waylynn stiffened.

"Funny how you think you know someone. How you think you can trust them." The bastard pointed the gun at her again and a rush of fury exploded behind Elliot's sternum. Her attacker wrenched her hair back, exposing her neck, and traced the column of her throat with the barrel. A thin scratch appeared in the path. "Then you discover what kind of monster they are. You know her secret, don't you, Dunham? You know what she's capable of."

Elliot lunged. Catching the shooter by surprise, he wrapped his hand around the gun's barrel with one hand and pushed Waylynn to the floor with the other, out of the way. A hard right hook ignited white streaks behind his eyelids. He went down on one knee. Slamming his elbow into her abductor's knee, he brought the arsonist down, too. But not for long. Another hit landed Elliot on his back and before he had a chance to dodge, the masked assailant was on top of him. One strike wrenched his head back into the white tile. A second darkened the edges of his vision.

His attacker dug his thumb into Elliot's bullet wound and a scream ripped from him like nothing before. A black haze descended over his vision, but he fought to stay conscious. He'd promised to protect her. He wouldn't fail her again. Pulling back his elbow, he gripped the masked assailant's shirt and launched his fist into the bastard's face.

Three gunshots exploded from over his head.

The man above him straightened, those dark brown eyes wide a split second before he collapsed to the tile beside Elliot. "He wasn't supposed to... kill Alexis."

Waylynn stared down at him, gun shaking between her hands, lips parted as though she couldn't believe what'd just happened. Stray stands of long, blond hair puffed with her strained exhales. She let go of the gun, metal meeting tile loud in his ears, as he pushed to his feet, then stumbled away from him. She shook her head. "I'm not a monster. I'm not a monster."

SHE'D KILLED HIM. The man who'd kidnapped her, strapped her to a chair and tried to burn her alive. And it'd been easy. It'd felt right. Because there was no way she was going to watch Elliot die right in front of her. She'd already lost too many people she cared about. Waylynn's hands still shook as she pushed hair out of her face. Red and blue patrol lights claimed her attention as the EMT beside her finished checking her blood pressure and other stats in the back of the ambulance. She didn't even know her attacker's name, didn't know why he'd targeted her. He'd known Alexis. That much was clear.

But it wasn't over. Not yet. The man who'd done those things tonight wasn't the same one who'd drugged her and killed Alexis. At least, not from the small bits and pieces she'd been able to recover of that night.

And Elliot…

She'd shot and killed someone with his own gun in Elliot's defense. What would he see when he looked at her after giving his statement to the Anchorage PD and the fire department? A monster as her attacker had claimed? Waylynn pulled the blanket around her tighter, ice freezing deep in her muscles. Odd, considering parts of Genism Corporation were still on fire.

"Dr. Hargraves." Officer Shea Ramsey, dressed in plain clothes, closed in on her from across the parking lot. Jeans, T-shirt, long curly hair burying her shoulders. Not on duty. "I heard everything on the radio. I'm glad you're okay."

Surprise rocketed Waylynn's pulse higher and she hopped down from the lip of the ambulance. "Officer Ramsey—"

"Shea, please." The officer motioned for her to sit, then took a seat beside her. A combination of pine and honey filled Waylynn's lungs. Officer Ramsey's caramel-colored eyes assessed the scene but watched the gurney being wheeled out the lab's front doors by two men from the coroner's office. "Have you talked to anybody about it yet? I mean, besides giving your statement to police about what happened? I can't imagine what you're feeling."

"No." Waylynn stared down at her hands. She'd never shot anyone before. Never taken a life despite popular belief. But it was inevitable, right? That was what she'd been trying to prove all these years with her research. The warrior gene turned normal, healthy, happy individuals into monsters in the blink of an eye. It was genetics. Fate. She just hadn't expected this day to come so soon. "What's there to talk about? I shot a man—" she swallowed around the bile working up her throat, the sight of so much blood still fresh in her mind "—to save my best friend. Elliot wouldn't be standing over there if I hadn't."

And she'd do it again.

"But he was your boss." Officer Ramsey's expression smoothed over. She narrowed in on Waylynn. "You worked beside him every day and you had no idea he wanted you dead?"

Air rushed from her lungs. No. That wasn't right. "What did you say?"

"They didn't tell you." Shea Ramsey ran a hand through that mass of hair and pushed off the back of the ambulance. She shifted her weight between both feet in agitated movements. "I'm sorry. I didn't mean... I thought you knew Dr. Matthew Stover was the attacker you shot. Uniformed officers are at his house now. He had surveillance footage of you, re-

cordings of calls from your cell phone, original news-
papers from your trial fifteen years ago."

The blanket fell from her shoulders as Waylynn
stood, attention on the gloved hand peeking out from
beneath the white sheet on the gurney. That hand had
started the fire meant to kill her, had pointed a gun
at her head. Couldn't be Matt's. He was her friend,
her supervisor, the one who'd given her a job when
she'd needed it the most. He'd run the warrior gene
trials based off her research, supported her, stood up
for her against the board members' threats to shut
down the study because of funding.

What had Elliot said before she'd put three bullets in her attacker? *You don't want her dead, which
means you need her for something. Or you know her.*

"Dr. Hargraves?" Officer Ramsey's voice sounded
far-off, distant, and it wasn't until Elliot barricaded
himself in front of her path that she realized she'd
bolted for the body on the gurney.

"Waylynn." His voice washed through her, threatened to distract her.

"I need to see his face." She angled herself to see
around his bandaged shoulder, to see the body as
the coroner loaded it into the back of his dark van.
Her breath sawed in and out of her lungs, a combination of smoke and man spreading through her system. No. Wasn't possible. Matt wouldn't have turned
on her like this. Her gaze snapped to Elliot's, those
mesmerizing gray eyes pulling her out of the haze
of confusion, and a tremor cartwheeled down her

spine. Would it always be like that? Would her body always want to give in to this unfiltered need to burrow into his arms whenever she laid eyes on him? Her heart beat too hard in her chest, but she met his stare straight on, hoping to appear stubborn and determined rather than out of her mind. "You said he didn't want to kill me. He knew me. You said that."

"Yes." He refused to budge. Sliding the hand of his uninjured arm up her neck, he framed her face. A muscle twitched in his jaw. "But seeing his face will only haunt you for the rest of your life. You have enough nightmares keeping you up at night. Trust me."

She did trust him. He'd saved her life. Three times now. Once by being willing to sacrifice himself for her safety. Nobody had ever done that before. Put her needs above theirs. Chancing one more glance at the gurney as the medical examiners shut the heavy van doors, Waylynn nodded. She closed the small space between them, the need for his touch so overwhelming. She buried her head in the hollow of his neck, exactly where she needed to be. A shiver rushed through her, warm tingles replacing the dread heating her blood. "Was it him? Was it Matt?"

"He was carrying his Genism Corporation ID. Must've used it to get access to the building after taking you from the crash site." Elliot wrapped his uninjured arm around her, pressed her tight against him. The steady rhythm of his heart helped control hers the more she focused on the sound, but the aftereffects of having taken a life still clung to her nervous system. "Explains how he knew how to disable the emergency system so the fire wouldn't be detected until it was too late."

A tremor shook through her from the top of her head and worked its way all the way down to her toes. A sob gushed from her lips and she held on to him tighter. "I was afraid he'd killed you."

"Not going to lie." Elliot planted a kiss at the crown of her head. "Being tasered and then shot sucks."

That earned him a laugh and suddenly, the fire, the betrayal, the explosion of bullets in her memory, it all slipped away. In such a short amount of time, Elliot had become the center of her universe. Her skin pimpled with awareness. Of him. Exhaust filled her lungs as the coroner's van pulled out of the lab's parking lot, but even with Matt Stover's body in the back, the nightmare wasn't over. Waylynn closed her eyes against the quick flash of memory from the scene at her apartment, but she couldn't shake the knowledge her boss hadn't killed Alexis. No. The man who'd forced her to write that confession at gunpoint was still out there. Maybe still targeting her.

"Your lawyer is here." Elliot's voice dropped into dangerous territory. Sure enough, Blake Henson climbed out of his town car and headed toward them. On the other side of the parking lot, two black SUVs pulled up alongside one of the ambulances. The Blackhawk Security team had arrived. With one last kiss planted on the top of her head, he released her. "Don't go anywhere. I'll be right back."

"Considering I'm wanted for murder, there aren't many places I can go." A smile tugged at one corner of her mouth as he met with the other members of his team. From what he'd told her about them during their long talks and beers after work, she assigned names to the operatives she spotted.

The one with the immovable expression had to be Sullivan Bishop, former Navy SEAL and the CEO and founder of the security firm. The tall, striking blonde…Waylynn guessed she had to be Kate Monroe, and her stomach sank a bit. Elliot had told her about one of Kate's patients who'd killed the psychologist's husband last year, but being back at work looked good on her. The others were easily identifiable. Elizabeth with her black leather jacket and fingernail polish and dark circles under her eyes. New mom. She'd met Vincent. Anthony Harris was most recognizable with a pair of aviator sunglasses and an armory strapped to his Kevlar. The woman at his side had to be his wife, the army investigator and newest recruit to the team, Glennon.

Elliot greeted each of them with a smile and a laugh, as though they were family. Considering he'd spent the last year with them day in and day out, she imagined they were the only family he had left. They protected each other, fought for each other, supported each other. A strange sensation spread from behind her sternum. What she wouldn't give to be part of a family like that again. To be loved.

"Dr. Hargraves, I came as soon as I'd heard the

situation over the police scanner." With his perfectly pressed Italian suit, Blake Henson ripped her back into the present moment. Cruiser lights deepened the fine lines around his mouth as the sun rose above the peaks of the mountains, but it was the light color of his eyes that paralyzed her from head to toe. Light blue. Just as she remembered from the flashes of that night in her apartment. "From what I understand, you're lucky to be alive. No permanent damage, I hope."

"Lucky. Right." Had nothing to do with the fact her next-door neighbor had put himself in the line of fire to protect her. Waylynn took a step back. "I'm sorry you had to come all the way down here, but as of two hours ago, I'm no longer an employee of Genism. The board decided to..." She paused around the building lump in her throat as her conversation with Matt before the crash replayed in her head. "They decided to let me go. So I guess I need to find another lawyer."

"Considering the circumstances and the fact your direct superior tried to murder you, I think I'll be able to negotiate with the board after all this damage is repaired." Blake Henson stretched out his hand, a business card between his index and middle finger. "Call me tomorrow and we'll work out the details to bring you back on board."

"Back?" She couldn't believe it. She took the card from the attorney, her attention automatically lowering to the back of his hand. Searching for a scar that wasn't there. Air rushed from her lungs and she relaxed a bit more. He might have the same-colored eyes as the man from her drugged memory, but she couldn't imagine a reason for Blake Henson to drug her, kill Alexis and frame Waylynn for murder. He was one of the company lawyers. While his job might involve keeping company activities and indiscretions from the press, he'd never looked at her twice in the ten years she'd worked for Genism. The past couple of days had messed with her head. She'd become suspicious of everyone. "Thank you."

"Everything okay?" Elliot's warmth tunneled through her clothing and straight to her bones as he wrapped his uninjured arm around her again. Relief spread like wildfire, but she drowned the urge to lean into him. Until they were alone.

"Get your rest, Dr. Hargraves. We'll talk tomorrow." Blake Henson turned back the way he'd come and climbed behind the wheel of his town car. Within a minute, he'd swerved out of the parking lot and disappeared.

"Everything's fine." At least, it would be. But right now, she wanted nothing more than to wash the smell of smoke from her clothes and gorge herself on real food. She studied the aftermath of the fire, the scorch marks and broken windows. An hour ago, she'd almost died in that building. Notching her chin higher, she tamped down another tremor shaking through her. "I'm ready for you to take me back to the cabin."

Chapter Nine

A broken woman made the most dangerous kind of warrior.

As Elliot led her back into the cabin, dried tear streaks cutting into the ash smudges on her face, he believed that 100 percent. She was a survivor. Always had been. And, damn, it looked good on her. Handing her the bag she'd packed at her apartment, he nodded toward the bathroom down the hall. Lucky the Blackhawk Security team had thought to grab it from the wreck. Otherwise, she might've been stuck wearing his MIT shirt again. He swallowed against the image of her dressed in nothing but that shirt earlier. "Why don't you go clean up? I'll round up something other than peanut-butter Oreos for—" he checked his watch "—breakfast, apparently."

Waylynn ran a hand over her arm, dead on her feet. She moved toward the kitchen. "You don't... You don't have to do that."

"You're dead on your feet, Doc." He gave in to her gravitational pull, closed the distance between them. Her perfume mixed with the smell of smoke became part of him. "You hired me to protect you. So I'm only going to say this once because I know you'll push yourself over the edge if I let you. I need you fed, cleaned up and in my bed within the hour. No argument."

Her mouth thinned as she crossed her arms and shifted her weight onto one foot. Defiance sparkled in those ocean-blue eyes as she hitched one knee to the side, every bit the brazen, smart-mouthed woman he couldn't get out of his head for a minute straight. Hell, her middle name was *defiance*. She'd pushed at his boundaries at every turn, buried herself beneath his skin to the point he didn't know how to get her out. Wasn't sure he wanted to, to be honest. "You realize I killed the last man who tried to boss me around, right? You sure you want to go down this road?" Sadness colored her voice.

She wasn't in the mood for joking. Elliot had embraced a special kind of darkness that allowed him to become whomever he needed to be in order to get the job done. He'd tricked dozens of targets into handing over their money, convinced them they were getting the better end of the deal, made them trust him. And she blew that all straight to hell when she looked at him like that. Like she was up for the challenge. And, damn, if that wasn't the sexiest thing he'd ever seen. "I think I can handle it."

"Be careful what you wish for." Leaning into him, she planted her palms on his chest and rose on tip-

toe. Her mouth leveled with his ear. His blood pressure shot into overdrive as she dropped her voice. "The devil comes disguised as everything you think you want."

Her fingertips brushed across the oversensitized skin down his arms as she headed for the bathroom, not a single glance back. His heart restarted as the bathroom door lock clicked into place. Seconds ticked by. A minute. He didn't know how long he stood there debating whether he should give in to the temptation to knock on that door. Elliot curled his fingers into fists. The moment he gave in, there would be no turning back. All too easily, he imagined her under the shower spray, nothing between them but rivulets of water, and every muscle he owned urged him to follow through.

No. He wouldn't barge in on her. She'd been through more than most the past two days. They both had, and he wasn't about to take advantage. He'd keep as much distance between them as he could in a tiny cabin. Which wasn't much. He forced his feet toward the kitchen instead of down the small hallway. Wrenching open the fridge door with his injured arm, he slammed a hand over the bullet wound in his shoulder. The pain kept him in the moment. Kept his mind on getting a meal together and nothing more.

The sizzle of olive oil and chicken in the pan drowned her approach, but the slight humidity crawling through the kitchen announced she'd finished in the shower before she appeared in his peripheral vision. "What's for breakfast?"

He didn't dare meet her gaze as he chopped asparagus, but everything about her—the way she spoke, how she brushed her hair behind her ears, even how perfectly she fit against him—drew him in. Always had. Tossing a pinch of salt and pepper into the skillet, Elliot faced her. And the air rushed from his lungs. The world's most exotic, alluring women had nothing on the blonde beauty in front of him. Baggy sweats and an oversize T-shirt hung off her lean frame but didn't detract from her overall attractiveness. If anything, his mind wandered to all the possibilities hiding under the thin fabric of her shirt. "Asparagus sweet potato chicken skillet."

He cleared his throat. Her hair hung in wet strands, accentuating the sharpness of her cheekbones and vividness in her stare. He tightened the grip on the knife in his hand.

And sliced his finger clean open.

Dropping the knife, Elliot reached for the hand towel hanging from the oven and wrapped his finger as fast as he could. "Damn it."

"Are you okay? Here, let me see." Waylynn hurried around the counter and took his hand in hers, mere inches between them. Smooth skin brushed against his as she studied the wound, but he barely noticed the pain. Every sense he owned had heightened in awareness. Because of her. Because of the concern etched into her expression, the sympathy in her voice. His heart thudded hard behind his ribs, almost as if the damn thing were trying to reach her. He'd kissed her once to prove there was nothing between them. No heat. No passion. It'd been rushed and rough. And he'd been dead wrong. There'd been nothing but heat. Nothing but passion and, hell, he couldn't stop thinking about that kiss now. Couldn't stop thinking about the next one either. "Doesn't look like you'll need stitches." She raised her head. "Something's burning."

He blinked to clear his head of her, her words registering through the Waylynn-induced haze. Damn it. Elliot ripped his hand out of hers and spun toward the skillet. Sure enough, black smoke and the scent of burned oil and chicken filled the kitchen. He twisted the knob to shut off the gas and exhaled hard. "I think we've had enough fires for one day. How about I go get us something?"

"There aren't any places open this early. How about you get your finger taken care of and I'll take care of this?" Waylynn brushed past him, that bright smile destroying the deepest part of him, the part that'd sworn off commitment in order to keep his freedom. She moved the skillet to another burner with a hot pad. Picking up the spatula he'd set beside the oven, she turned back to him and pointed with it. "Go. I promise not to burn your cabin down. Although, it wouldn't be hard because it's so small."

"I'm sensing some hostility toward my top-secret safe house." He pulled a first-aid kit out of the top drawer of the kitchen and wrapped a bandage around the wound. "It's not that bad. Come on. Where else can you say you almost got trampled by a moose and her young?"

No reaction. She pushed the burned mess around the skillet with the spatula. Her hands shook and she set the utensil onto the granite. "I'm sorry. I didn't mean… I appreciate everything you've done for me. I do. I've been through all of this before when I was accused of killing my father, but I—"

"Wasn't expecting you'd have to shoot your boss? I can't imagine what you're feeling, Doc." Elliot tossed the first-aid kit back into the drawer and bumped it closed with his hip. "I never said thank you, did I? Without you, I probably wouldn't be standing here. Also, how in the hell did a geneticist beat the crap out of me?"

Waylynn stepped into him. Reaching for his wounded shoulder, she brushed her fingers over the fresh gauze and tape. "Matt's been involved with MMA fighting for years. Said it kept him in shape. I never considered he'd… I never thought he'd be the one to turn on me." She raised her gaze to his, her hand framing his jaw and one of the bruises on the side of his face. The small muscles there twitched in response to her touch. "I'm sorry, Elliot. For everything. You wouldn't have been beaten, shot or almost burned alive if it weren't for me."

"Don't forget tasered." He sure wouldn't. He snaked his uninjured arm around the small of her back, pressing her against him. Right where she belonged. His smile died. She blamed herself. For all of it. That was the kind of person she was. Forced to grow up too fast after losing her parents, taking on more responsibility than a fifteen-year-old should've had to have dealt with. She'd lost an entire childhood—like he had—but she felt responsible because he bet that was the only way for her to keep it together. "Waylynn, you're not responsible for any of this. Not for the crash, not what happened to me. You *are* responsible for Matt Stover's death but nobody's going to hold that against you. Whoever killed Alexis Jacobs and got your boss to do their dirty work did this. And I'm going to find them."

"Right. A psychopath is targeting me because I like puppies and rainbows." A humorless laugh escaped her mouth. She traced a seam in his shirt with her thumb but backed out of his reach. After threading one hand through her hair, she crossed her arms beneath the baggy shirt, accentuating her small frame. Her attention traveled to the front door as she bit her thumbnail. Color drained from her face as she steadily walked toward it and secured the dead bolt. "I feel as though I'm losing my mind. Two days ago, I got a message from Alexis to meet me at my apartment, and now she and my boss are dead."

Her tightly held control had started to crack.

"You're safe here." Spinning her into him, he forced Waylynn to look him in the eye. The outright terror in her expression raised his protective instinct.

"I will protect you. No matter the cost. Physically, mentally, I will do anything to keep you safe."

"I know you will, but for how long? Another day? A week? It could take months to identify whoever framed me, Elliot." She rolled her lips between her teeth, her gaze drifting to the front door again. To double-check the lock?

"However long it takes, Doc." He pulled her into him, those blue eyes locking on his mouth for the briefest of moments. "I'm not going anywhere."

BEING IN HER life was a death sentence. That was clear now. First her father, then her mother. Now Alexis and Matt. Waylynn forced herself to take a step back, forced herself to take her eyes off his mouth, and suppressed the chaotic need burning inside her to stay in his arms. She couldn't let Elliot be next. Couldn't let him become a victim of her genetic code down the line. He was too important. He was…everything.

Her blood heated at the realization. Holy mother of peanut-butter Oreos. Her throat dried. She'd always found him attractive, charming, funny. But now? Now, she couldn't stop thinking about how much time she'd wasted over the last year. How she'd hidden her crush, how much she looked forward to seeing him every day after work for that beer. The way they recited bad country songs to make each other laugh. They'd almost died in that fire. He'd been shot trying to save her life. In the blink of an eye, she could've lost him forever. And she wasn't going to waste another minute. "Kiss me."

Waylynn didn't wait for an answer. Interlocking her fingers around the back of his neck, she crushed her body against his. Hard muscle pressed into her as he wrapped her with his uninjured arm. She notched her mouth higher to meet his lips as she came up on her toes. The difference between their sizes was laughable, but somehow, it worked. Everything about Elliot Dunham defied the fantasy she'd built in her head of the perfect man over the years, when she'd allowed herself to imagine a long-term relationship with a partner. His occupation, his height, even the color of his eyes. But right now, if only for tonight— no, forever—she wanted him. "Am I hurting you?"

"If you stop, I'll be in a lot more pain than I am right now," he said.

A smile stretched her mouth thin. She'd tried to stay in control for the last two days, tried not to let herself splinter, tried not to let him see how much she needed him. But it'd all been in vain as he slipped his tongue into her mouth. She had no control. Not when it came to him. Sliding her palm down his stomach, she reveled in the strong, muscled ridges and valleys beneath her fingers. His heartbeat changed. Sped up. She'd done that. Despite his insistence of keeping things between them professional, she'd elicited a reaction from him. Because he'd been made for her. No other man had ignited this craving to be touched, to be loved, and she couldn't get enough.

Pressing her back against the counter, Elliot caged her between him and cold granite, the difference in battling temperatures fighting for dominance. He kissed her deeper, faster, and the ridiculous-sized cabin, the investigation, the fact she'd killed her boss to save his life less than two hours ago vanished. There was only him.

And with a deep trail of kisses down her throat, he had the power to break her. Elliot intertwined his fingers with hers, then raised her raw knuckles to his mouth. One by one, he kissed the wounds, sending small electric pulses through her nervous system. "I don't care what that bastard said. You're not a monster, Doc. You're a survivor. Always have been. Only now it's written all over your body."

I'm not a monster. Her words as she'd pulled that trigger drained the burning heat smoldering beneath her skin. She didn't want to think about that. Not now, not after he'd just started to make her feel. Monsters killed. Deep inside, everyone had the potential to kill, but according to her own research, the odds had increased for her the moment she'd been born. One day she could be Dr. Jekyll, the next Ms. Hyde. "How can you be sure?"

"I've met real monsters, Waylynn. You might've shot a man a few hours ago, but I'll tell you right now, you're not one of them. You're kind, you're generous, you put others first and strive to do what's right. You came back for me in the middle of the fire at the cost of putting your own life in danger." He smoothed his thumb across her knuckles. "And you can either fight that fact or accept it. You can let that fear control you or take the control and move on with your life. Those are your choices."

What she wouldn't give to believe every word out of his kiss-swollen mouth, but the truth remained. She couldn't outrun genetics. Nobody could. Tears burned in her lower lash line, thick salt coating the back of her throat and behind her teeth. Twisting away, she put as much distance as she could between them in the limited amount of space. The fantasy she'd built up inside her head was just that. A fantasy. How could she have been so stupid to let it tint the real world? "There is no choice, Elliot. Not for me."

"Why not?" A strong hand wrapped around her arm and spun her back into him. "Why don't you get to be happy?"

"I have the warrior gene!" Waylynn clamped her hand over her mouth, the tears finally falling. She couldn't hide the truth anymore. Couldn't live with the weight by herself. Swiping the back of her hand across her face, she sniffled. Control. She forced a weak smile. "So you see? Even if we find the person responsible for framing me, I don't get a happily-ever-after, Elliot. I don't get to spend the rest of my life with the man I've fallen in love with. I don't get to have the family I've always dreamed of having. Because one day, my DNA will force me to turn on them. Just like my father's did."

Elliot suddenly seemed so much…bigger as a sharp edge cooled the gray of his eyes. Dropping his hand, she lost the little bit of body heat she'd been able to hold on to since shooting Matt Stover. Panic flared the longer he stared down at her, unreadable, unmovable. What did he think of her now? What did he see? His throat worked to swallow. "The man you've fallen in love with?"

There were two kinds of secrets. The one she'd kept from others and the one she'd kept from herself. But she couldn't shoulder either. Not anymore. She wasn't sure when it'd happened. Maybe that first time he'd waited for her after work with a beer and a smile. Could've been the moment he'd come running to help her after she'd discovered Alexis in the tub and screamed. Or was it when he'd taken that bullet back at the crash scene to distract her boss from kidnapping her? Did it matter? Wiping her face, a strained laugh escaped past her lips. "Come on now. You're a private investigator, remember? You're trained to read people. Isn't that what you said? You had to have seen it. I'm not that good of a liar."

Elliot blinked, running his palms down his face. Turning away from her, he kept his body language neutral, but none of that screamed *reciprocating feelings* and her stomach sank.

What did she expect? He'd made himself perfectly clear. Nothing would happen between them. Living in the commune, spending over a year in an Iraqi prison, being in a committed relationship. They were all the same to him. Prisons. Barriers to his own happiness. She'd cut herself off from any kind of human interaction past a professional level in a sick attempt to protect others. Her throat tightened as rejection took hold. Maybe she should've been more concerned about herself. "Elliot—"

"I don't care," he said.

Everything inside her shattered.

Smudges of ash darkened the angles of his jaw, hardening his expression. Elliot shook his head. "Wait. That came out wrong. I don't care about your genetics, Doc. I don't care if some gene changes you into someone else down the road. I know who you are." He closed in on her, the scent of smoke and man filling her lungs as he took her beat-up hands in his. "Every second I get to spend with you is better than losing you altogether."

She swallowed back the salty taste in her mouth. "What?"

"You're going to make me say it all over again, aren't you?" That gut-wrenching smile of his rocketed her blood pressure higher. In an instant, it vanished. Smoothing his thumbs across her knuckles again, he softened his stance. "You've got blood on your hands, but I don't see a monster when I look at you. I see my best friend. The woman who means more to me than anyone else in my life. The woman I'll do anything to keep for myself."

"You're not scared of what I might turn into." Not a question. He had to have read her father's file, read hers and her mother's statements after his body had been recovered. Nathan Hargraves had terrorized his family until the day he'd died. Elliot understood the risks, yet he still wanted her. The slight tenderness of her lips from his kiss was proof, wasn't it? He was willing to break the rule he'd set between them: no emotional attachments. For her. "You don't have to do this. We can stay friends like you wanted. We'll figure it out—"

"What's life without a bit of risk?" Elliot shrugged with his uninjured shoulder.

She couldn't contain the smile spreading her lips thin, fisting her fingers in his shirt to drag his mouth down to hers. Grazing her bottom lip along his, she nipped at him before pulling away. "Don't say I didn't warn you."

Her gut clenched at another sight of that tingling-inducing smile as he pressed his mouth to hers. Her laugh broke free at the sound of her stomach growling. Right. They hadn't eaten anything in… She didn't know how long. Waylynn released him. "Well, that certainly ruins the mood."

"Nah." Elliot interlaced his fingers through hers and flipped her palm toward the not-so-high ceiling. With his gaze locked on hers, he kissed the overly sensitive skin along the inside of her wrist. "Just postpones it a bit."

Her nerve endings burned with awareness. Nearly a lifetime of fear for the future drained from her system. Because of him. He'd given her reason not to escape the darkness. Instead, maybe she could learn to love herself there with his help. "All right. Food. Sleep. Then making out."

Elliot winked at her as he started working on saving the chicken and oil in the pan one-handed. "It's good to have priorities."

Chapter Ten

She'd fallen asleep in his arms, both of them too exhausted to do much else after gorging themselves on the bits of chicken and vegetables he'd managed to save. It hadn't taken more than a few minutes for him to fall asleep with her safe in his arms, her clean, flowery scent clinging to his shirt and boxers. Hints of her perfume filled his lungs now, but, when Elliot reached across the sheets, he discovered it to be a figment of his imagination. The bed was empty. Sunlight streamed through the pane of the massive triangle-shaped window out the back of the cabin. He checked his watch. Noon. He'd been asleep for close to eight hours. And, hell, it'd been the best sleep of his life as far as he was concerned.

Some guys just couldn't handle a bullet to the shoulder.

Him being one of them.

Running a hand through his hair, he threw his legs over the side of the bed and pushed to his feet. Strapping his arm into the sling the paramedics had given him at the scene after treating him, Elliot rolled back his shoulder to stretch the injury. With pain came clarity. His muscles protested as he moved toward the stairs, but the deafening silence pulled him deeper into the small space. "Doc?"

No answer.

Cold hardwood creaked under his weight as he hit the bottom step. The smell of coffee fought to distract him, but his heart jumped into his throat as he caught sight of her. Lean muscle and strength stretched and contorted into shapes he'd never seen a human body execute. Shadows deepened the ridges and valleys across her exposed midsection and back around her sports bra. Neon leggings left little to the imagination as she balanced precariously on both hands—no support—and lifted the crown of her head toward her toes in an impossible backbend. He'd never seen anything like it. Never seen anything quite like her.

How could someone so beautiful, so strong, believe she'd turn into a monster? Elliot rested his uninjured shoulder against the wall, watching the sweep of her arms and legs in a hypnotic dance.

Floating her legs back to the floor, Waylynn exhaled hard as she turned. She jumped with a small scream, a hand on her collarbones, as she spotted him across the room. She pulled wireless headphones from her ears. "How long have you been standing there like a creepy stalker?"

"Long enough to think you've been possessed by

a poltergeist. I considered calling a priest to exorcize it from your body." It was only when she reached for a towel off the back of the bar stool that he noticed the sprawl of papers and his laptop open on the counter.

"If there's one thing I learned cramming through the night during my doctoral program, it was exercise helps me focus." Waylynn set her headphones on the counter. Small beads of sweat built in her hairline, the bruise along her jawline from where that bastard Dr. Stover had backhanded her more purple than black now.

It'd been a damn good thing Waylynn had gotten to him first. Elliot had wanted nothing more than to finish the job himself after what her boss had put her through. Rage flooded through him at the vile memory, but he forced himself in check. Hell, maybe he needed to exercise, too. The Genism Corporation logo caught his attention on the stack of papers she'd left on the counter. He spidered his fingers over the top one and turned it toward him. Handwritten notes detailed possible suspects within the company, starting at the very top, then navigating to the bottom on what looked like official letterhead. "Look at you taking up the private investigator mantle. Any leads?"

"If I go with the theory someone within Genism wanted to hide the results of our warrior gene trials, no. There are too many suspects to count, and it would take months to sift through it all. Every executive had reason to protect the lab. Money, reputation, the fact Genism is in direct competition with a few other labs for pharmaceutical company contracts. Not to mention military contracts. The list goes on." She wiped the towel across her collarbones with one hand and moved another sheet of paper out from under the stack with the other. "The only thing I'm certain about is whoever killed Alexis gave Dr. Stover my DNA results so I would be labeled a monster capable of murder. With my past, it wasn't hard, but framing me didn't do the job, so they escalated to direct attack. I just don't know how they got that DNA information. I assigned numbers to each volunteer in the study, including myself when I submitted my blood work. There weren't any names on the dozens of reports I filed. No way they could've read a result and assigned it to a specific subject. Matt didn't have access to that information."

"You had to have recorded them somewhere," he said. "Companies like Genism cover their asses. Did the subjects sign releases, legal documents?"

"Yeah. Of course they did. If the suspect works in Genism's legal department, they'd have access to all of the waivers with subjects' personal information and the numbers I'd assigned. All they'd have to do is look at the results for a match. Which narrows it down to about…one hundred people with access to that information." Her shoulders deflated. Draping the towel onto the back of the chair, she shuffled through the paperwork searching for another hand-drawn diagram and picked it up. An employee flow chart. In her next breath, she tossed it back to the counter. "I take that back. That does not narrow the suspect pool."

Only one name came to mind.

"What about your lawyer? What's his name again?" The SOB who'd dared put his hand on her at the police station after her interrogation.

"Blake Henson? He didn't have a scar when he handed me his business card at the crime scene. Believe me, I checked. Has to be someone else." Waylynn bit her bottom lip before running one hand through her hair. The weight of her gaze pressurized the air in his lungs as he studied the almost-completed list of personnel she'd constructed from memory. "Are we going to talk about what's on your computer?"

"It's not mine. I'm holding it for a friend." A laugh rumbled through him at her smile, but he knew exactly what she was referring to. The file folder. The only file folder on his desktop. Smoothing his uninjured hand against the counter, he straightened. "How'd you get into it?"

"I made it through twenty years of school. It wasn't hard to guess your password." Maneuvering the laptop toward him, she presented the individual files he'd been collecting the day he joined the Blackhawk Security team. Coworkers. Clients. People he'd investigated for his clients. Every shred of their lives was in that file. Bank records, mortgage paperwork, daily schedules, family, affairs, where their children went to school. Everything he needed to know to do his job sat in a password-protected folder only he'd had access to. Until now. Okay, he hadn't needed it all, but knowing the people he came into contact with—sometimes on a daily basis—fed his inner survivalist. Never knew when a bit of blackmail could help the situation. "I didn't read them, if that's what you're worried about. My only question is where's my file?"

"You really want to know?" Hesitation showed in her gaze and he couldn't help but smile. He could draw this out, have some much-needed fun after what'd happened over the last few days, but he tapped his index finger against his temple. "In my head."

"You don't have a physical or digital file?" she asked.

"Nope." Rounding the counter, he tugged a cabinet door open and took down two mugs. Seconds ticked by. Maybe a full minute as he poured coffee into the mugs and offered her one. Black. The way she liked it. He handed her a cupful. "Why? Are you feeling left out?"

"No, it's just… You've run background checks on the people you work with, even your boss, and, from the looks of it, anyone who might've even road raged at you on the freeway." Sipping on her coffee, she steered her focus back to the computer screen. "Why not me?"

Elliot took a gulp of dark liquid, reveling in the burn down his throat. Settling his lower back against the opposite counter, he increased the space between them. A lie would be easy. He hadn't gotten around to it. He knew everything he needed to know about her. She wasn't interesting enough to investigate. Lie. Lie. Lie. If he was being honest with himself, there was only one reason he hadn't dug into her personal life as he'd done with everyone else he came into contact with. He couldn't stand the thought of losing *her*.

"Because you're the last person I think of at night when I go to sleep and the first person I think of when I wake up." Setting his coffee on the granite, he rubbed the muscle by the hole in his shoulder. He stepped around the counter. "You're the only woman I know who can recite every bad '90s country song from memory and make a crappy day better with a single smile." His body craved hers as he slowly closed the distance between them. "You're the most intelligent, beautiful, sexy and puzzling scientist I know and I guess, when it came right down to it—" Elliot lowered his mouth over hers "—I didn't want to spoil the surprise."

"How thoughtful of you." She notched her chin higher to meet his mouth. "So what now?"

Sliding his uninjured arm across her lower back, he hiked her into his chest. Ferocious need raged through him. Dangerous. Intoxicating. Lethal to the single rule he'd laid out for himself when he'd gotten out of Iraq: no emotional attachments. But, right now, the thought of losing freedom to this woman only strengthened that need more. "Well, we've eaten and caught up on some sleep. I think we need to stick to our plan and make out."

"I do love a man with a plan." Waylynn intertwined her fingers with his and tugged him up the stairs after her.

He'd broken his rules. For her.

The thought coaxed a smile as she set her ear against his bare chest. Ridges and valleys of muscle flexed beneath her as she planted a kiss on his sternum. What she wouldn't give to stay here forever. Forget Alexis's murder. Forget that'd she'd been framed for killing her own assistant. Forget finding the person responsible or the fact she'd been let go from the only job she'd ever cared about. How much more did they have to go through before giving up was okay? How much more before she got her life back?

Resting her chin on his sternum, she studied the details of his face and filled with heat all over again. Her pulse hammered behind her ears. She loved him. She'd known it before, but she was sure of it now more than ever. What other reason was there for having such a strong reaction to him? The last few hours in this bed had been everything and more. Not only physically but mentally, emotionally. For a little while, she'd forgotten the need to survive and…lived. And the idea she'd have to go the rest of her life as just friends from here on out threatened to shred her apart on the inside. Wasn't going to happen. They'd forged something new, something better, stronger than before. Not even he could deny that.

"I know what you're thinking." Slowly, he traced a fingertip over her spine and a shudder of pleasure washed through her. She squirmed against him, the wrinkled sheets pulling away from them as she narrowly avoided his injured shoulder. "How in the world did we go this long without jumping each other?"

She set her forehead against his chest and planted a soft kiss over his heart. "More like how did we do it all those times without tearing your stitches."

Following the bruise pattern along her jaw, he kept his touch light. Darkness chased the desire from his eyes in an instant—most likely brought on by the memory of how she'd gotten the bruise in the first place—and she ran her hand through his beard in an attempt to keep him in the here and now. "Even if I did, it would have been worth it."

"I'm glad you think so, but sooner or later, we've got to leave this cabin." Waylynn slipped her hand over the back of his, then brought it to her mouth as he'd done downstairs before she rolled away from the comfort of his warmth. Wrapping one of the sheets around her body, she threw her legs over the bed to stand, but was pulled back to the mattress. A shout escaped from between her lips as she fell straight into his arms. He hovered above her, that gut-wrenching smile raising her desire all over again.

"I've got food storage under this bed like you wouldn't believe. We don't have to go anywhere." He placed a kiss on the tip of her nose, her senses going wild. Would it always be like this between them? This undeniable excitement whenever he touched her? "But if you insist, we can always hook up the cabin to the SUV and travel, get out of Anchorage."

"You're joking, right?" He couldn't be serious. "What about your deal with Blackhawk Security? Won't the men you conned out of their money come after you if Sullivan stops paying?"

"Can't come after me if they can't find me," he said. "I've still got contacts and cash. We could change our names, hit the road. Never look back."

Waylynn sat up, twisted around to face him. She clutched the sheets around her, the heat between them draining from her veins every second he actually considered picking up and leaving. Had that been his plan all along? Pay his debt, then disappear? Would she have come home from work one day to find his cheap camping chair on the front porch empty and his belongings gone? "You've thought this through."

"I've never been good staying in one place," he said.

Her brain automatically searched for the sarcastic remark that would sweep all this talk of him leaving under the rug, but nothing came to mind. "I don't know what to say."

"Say you'll come with me." He slipped his hand

into hers. "You've got nothing left here, Doc. Your family is gone, the lab's board of directors let you go. And don't forget the killer who put a target on your back. Say yes."

He was right. She had nothing left here. The realization tightened the grip she had on the sheets. She opened her mouth to answer, but a high-pitched ringing shot her blood pressure higher. Waylynn exhaled hard as he reached for his phone beside the bed. Saved by the bell.

"It's Kate. I asked her to construct a profile on this guy. Hopefully she has something useful." He shoved off the bed and answered the phone. "Go for Dunham."

Leveraging the phone between his uninjured shoulder and jaw, he pushed his legs into his jeans, then disappeared down the stairs, only tendrils of his conversation audible from this spot where she'd gotten a glimpse of the future. "When?"

Leave Anchorage? Reaching into her overnight bag, she pulled fresh clothing from the bottom, ignoring the heavy weight inside, and dressed as fast as she could. What were they supposed to do? Ignore the fact she'd been framed for murder by running? She was still the main suspect in Alexis Jacobs's investigation. Dr. Stover's attempt on her life had only derailed the case, not solved it. Anchorage PD wouldn't let her leave the city, let alone leave the state. They'd issue a warrant for her arrest and, given the theory somebody from the lab had started this nightmare, she wouldn't get far. Genism Corporation was one of the largest genetics laboratories in the country. Their reach—their resources—extended further than Waylynn could ever imagine.

She didn't want to spend the rest of her life looking over her shoulder.

Beeping from Elliot's security panel rang loud in her ears as he stepped outside onto the cabin's small front porch. The door clicked closed, leaving her alone for the first time in days.

She'd grown up here, built her life, built a career. She'd stared down an entire city of citizens convinced she'd murdered her father and held her head high and her middle finger higher. She deserved to be happy here, had given everything to this town. Could she really give that up?

No.

Not because some psychopath had destroyed her life's work, and not because the man she'd fallen for had his own ideals of freedom. If Elliot wanted to leave Anchorage behind, leave *her* behind... Her throat threatened to close in on itself. She'd survive. Just as she'd survived everything else in her life. Making her way downstairs, she dived back into the work she'd started before she'd given Elliot everything she had left. She could rebuild her research. It might take another decade, she might never find another lab to take her on and finance the trials she needed, but she could do this. She'd done it once. She could do it again. If she could get to Genism's server, she might be able to salvage what was left of her career.

Typing in her login and password to the lab's remote access, she nearly cried from relief. The board hadn't shut down her access yet. Her trial notes, her research, patient results, everything was there. But hadn't Matt said the files were damaged during the break-in? Scrambling to save ten years' worth of research as fast as she could, Waylynn swept a hand through her hair to fight the anxiety climbing up her throat. The lab's IT department might've been waiting to see if she'd try her access. Even though she'd poured her soul into this work, the research technically belonged to Genism. She couldn't copy and paste it into her next job, but she could use it to rebuild. She didn't have to start from scratch as she'd feared. Shoving Elliot's thumb drive into the port on the laptop, she waited for the device's window to load.

Then froze.

There was only one other file on the drive. Labeled with Nathan Hargraves's name. The thumbnail detailed the contents. Her father's police report. Her stomach dropped, the edges of her vision darkening as she held her breath. Elliot had lied to her. He'd claimed he hadn't investigated her past. Waylynn swallowed through the gravitational urge to run. He'd obviously read the report. Had he discovered who'd really killed her father?

The security system announced his opening the front door, and a rush of cool morning air raised the hairs on the back of her neck. Or was that the weight of his attention drilling into her spine? "We've got a problem."

Waylynn clicked off the thumb drive's window, leaving only Genism's server screen visible on the laptop. After everything they'd been through, after what they'd shared upstairs in that bed, why would he lie to her about his own private investigation? Her heartbeat thundered behind her ears. The police hadn't been able to solve her father's murder, but Elliot wasn't police. He wasn't held back by the same laws, wasn't scared to cross the line when it came to solving a case. And it wasn't in his nature to let things lie when the evidence ran out. She trusted him with her life, thought she loved him. He was good and intelligent and her best friend. But if he'd read that file, then he knew the truth Anchorage PD hadn't been able to prove without the murder weapon and there was nothing she could do about it. Bile worked up her throat. Her body felt heavy, weighed down, but she stood strong.

Crossing her arms across her midsection, she sat on the edge of the bar stool and fought the nervousness blazing through her. "Just one problem? Last time I counted, we had more than that."

Tossing his phone onto the counter beside the laptop and her headphones, Elliot ran a hand down his thick beard. Those hands had touched her oversensitized skin less than an hour ago, had awakened things inside her she'd fully believed she couldn't have. He'd saved her life—twice—but, more important, had saved her future. A future with a man who wasn't afraid of what she might become.

She studied him. No smile. No sarcastic remark. Pushing away from the bar stool, she closed in on him as his fisted hands shook at his sides. The tendons between his shoulders and neck strained to the point she again thought he might tear open his stitches. Panic flared hot and bright behind her sternum. "Elliot? What happened?"

He locked violent gray eyes on her. "Someone broke into Liz's home and stole the hard drive."

Chapter Eleven

The bastard had gone after his team, threatened Elizabeth Dawson, her family. Blackhawk's network security analyst and her baby had been able to get out of the house while Liz's significant other, Braxton, had taken shots at the SOB. Police were at the house now, taking statements, but this could've gone a whole other direction. Elliot pushed a hand through his hair. Damn it. He hadn't meant for this. Hadn't meant for any of this when he'd handed over that drive.

"Is she okay?" Concern deepened the lines around Waylynn's mouth as she sank against the bar stool again. "She has a baby—"

"Everyone is fine. Just a bit shook up." He said the words more for himself than to comfort her. Anything to keep himself from charging down there, leaving Waylynn unprotected and tracking the suspect down himself. "Kate's with them at the house. Wanted me to know they didn't mention the hard drive to the police."

Waylynn nodded. "Genism would've claimed intellectual property and taken the drive before we could read what was on it. Probably destroyed the device to hide whatever was on it to prevent a leak."

"Yeah, well, Liz hasn't been able to get much other than the lab's logo off any of the files yet, so I'm not sure how much use the drive is going to be." How the man who'd broken in knew about it in the first place was a mystery. Alexis Jacobs's apartment had been searched and cleaned before they'd gotten there. Could've been the same perp who'd broken into the assistant's apartment and Liz's home. "But it proves Alexis broke company policy. Something in your work together was important enough for her to risk her job and a possible lawsuit. The killer has to know exactly what's on that hard drive and wants it enough to kill for. Otherwise, why go after it at all?"

"Your stitches are bleeding." Waylynn crossed the small space between them, her geranium scent tempting him to pull her back up the stairs. She smoothed her fingers over the bandage and peeled back a corner, but the mutual pleasure they'd shared less than an hour ago had cooled. Significantly. Maneuvering him to the bar stool, she turned her back to him. "Sit down. I'll grab the first aid kit."

He hadn't noticed the blood, his head too wrapped up in the investigation, in her. Elliot slid his hand around hers, turning her into him. "We're going to catch this guy, Doc. He'll never touch you again."

"I know." Her voice hollowed as she ran a hand

through her hair, a nervous habit she'd formed over the last few days. "But how many more people are going to get hurt in the process? First Alexis. Then Matt. Now the people on your team are in danger. Their families. I…" Waylynn pulled her hand out of his. "I've lost everyone close to me. I can't lose you, too."

"First off, I've been doing this job long enough to know the risks, and so has my team. They're prepared for the worst. Trust me when I say they can take care of themselves. The son of a bitch was lucky Braxton didn't put a hole in him for coming near his girls." Elliot stood, bringing her in to him. "And, second, you're not going to lose me. I made you a promise and I intend to keep it. No matter the cost."

"Okay," she said. "Then I can tell you our next move. If the killer knows what's on that drive, it makes sense that he knew Alexis. Maybe had a relationship with her."

"I'm impressed." He focused on the laptop as she pulled away from him and sat on the bar stool. "Did she ever mention a boyfriend? An ex? Someone she spent a lot of time with at the lab?"

"Not that I remember, but the company looks down on interoffice relationships." Waylynn's fingers hit the keyboard in rapid succession and the screen flickered to life. "She wouldn't have told me she was seeing someone in the lab, but I was able to log into Genism's servers to recover all my research that'd been destroyed. If your teammate wasn't able to decrypt the hard drive before it was stolen, we might be able to find out what Alexis stored on it by reviewing her server history. So far the medical records I was able to access through the server haven't turned anything up on recent hand injuries, but I'm searching for Alexis's trail now."

Anticipation burned through him. They'd been waiting for a break in the investigation, waiting to see what Waylynn's assistant had died for. Elliot forced himself to breathe evenly. He'd been waiting to find the bastard who'd dared come after his woman. Because she was his to protect, his responsibility. But he didn't believe in luck. Didn't believe in coincidence either. Her boss had gone as far as to put a tracking device in Waylynn's phone in order to take her out himself. There was no telling how far the lab executives she'd dedicated ten years of her life to would go to protect themselves and the company. "When did you find out you still have access to the servers?"

"After you went outside." Her fingers stilled on the keyboard, but she didn't look up at him. "This isn't going to define the rest of my life. The pain, death and violence have been threatening to pull me under, but I'm going to keep my head above water. I'm going to rebuild my life and I'm going to rebuild my research." She nodded once. "I've done it once. I can do it again. You showed me that."

Damn straight she could. And he'd be right there at her side. Her biggest supporter. No matter how long it took, he'd help her rebuild everything she'd lost and more. "Did you practice that in front of the mirror?"

"Maybe a little." Her laugh cut through him and in the span of three seconds, it was the most exhilarating and life-altering experience of his life.

He loved this woman. Down to his bones, couldn't live the rest of his life without her, without loving her. Waylynn Hargraves was the strongest, most fearless woman he'd ever known. She'd stared death in the face and laughed. She'd decided fear wouldn't control her as it would so many others in the same situation and he couldn't take his eyes off her. Possessiveness exploded through him. He reached out, curling a strand of hair around his finger. Whatever that meant for their future—if they had a future together—he didn't know. But he was willing to give it a try. Screw the past. His parents, the prison guards. They were nothing like the woman in front of him. She wouldn't try to imprison him, wouldn't betray him. She didn't have the heart. "If I haven't made it clear before, if you do ever end up killing someone, I'll help you bury the evidence."

"Just what every woman wants to hear." Another flash of that brilliant smile. The laptop beeped, bringing her focus back to the screen. "I've got it. Looks like Alexis was singling out certain subjects and separating them into a new file."

"What made those subjects special?" Elliot rested his uninjured arm against the back of the chair and leaned in over her shoulder. Her breathing patterns changed and he couldn't help but revel in the knowledge that his closeness was the reason. He'd done that to her, made her breath hitch, affected the pulse at the base of her neck.

"I don't know. They're labeled by their trial numbers I assigned to each volunteer. No names, but every one of them were positive for the warrior gene." Waylynn leaned back in the chair. "I won't be able to match them without the waivers I handed over to the legal department when the subjects applied to be part of the trial."

"Can you access those files from the servers, too?" he asked.

"It's worth a try." Waylynn clicked off the current screen and slid her fingers across the track pad. A minute—maybe two—later, she shook her head. "I don't have access to those files. We'd need someone from Legal to get them for us, but I know someone who might be able to help." She rolled her lips between her teeth, then headed for the stairs without another word. Within thirty seconds, she hit the bottom step, holding a small white rectangle between her fingers. "Blake Henson gave me his card back at the scene. He wanted me to call him today to work out reinstating me with the lab, but he might be willing to help us if we explain someone in his department is a murderer."

"Let me get this straight." Elliot ran a hand down his beard. "We're going to ask an employee paid to protect the company he works for to hand over confidential corporate documents to help our illegal investigation."

"You think it's a bad idea?" Uncertainty deepened the lines between her eyebrows as she studied the business card, and damn, he had to fight the urge to smooth them away.

"No, I just wanted to make sure I heard you right." He closed the distance between them. "We'll find him. No matter how long it takes or how many different plans we need to come up with. We're in this together."

"So you're not going to try to sneak out of the cabin in the middle of the night to follow evidence again, then?" she asked.

"I knew you were going to hold that against me." He framed her jaw with one hand and moved his mouth over hers lightly. An explosion of that unchecked need pressed his body against hers. "But, no. For better or worse, you're stuck with me."

Her face lit up and every muscle he owned coiled tight. She rose up on her toes, leveling that intoxicating blue gaze with his. Cocking her head to the side, she wrapped her arms around the back of his neck, careful to avoid the hole in his shoulder. "It'll probably be for worse."

A laugh rumbled through him. Then he kissed her. Hard. Fast. It was too late to turn back now. She'd claimed him from the inside out and he would have handed his soul over willingly. He came up for air but couldn't suppress the wild addiction he had for her flooding through him. "I knew that the moment I met you."

WELL, THEY WEREN'T best friends anymore.

The haze surrounding her brain had taken a stronger hold than before, to the point she'd lost track of time. Nothing remained but him and his clean, masculine scent in her lungs. Three days. That was all it'd taken to change her life, to discover a connection stronger than the one her genetics had forged on her future. She wasn't sure how long they'd stood there, his mouth on hers, her pressed against him. Stepping back for air, Waylynn flitted her fingers over the edge of the gauze taped to his shoulder. They'd gotten distracted. She set her palms against his chest, his heartbeat strong beneath her touch, and backed off. "As much as I'd love to make out with you all day, we need to change your bandage, then call my lawyer."

"Forget it. Let it get infected." He moved to close the space she'd put between them.

She countered his approach, a rush of gut-clenching delirium threatening to help her get lost in him all over again, but she wouldn't wait for whoever'd framed her to find her first. "That was a nice way of me saying we need to brush our teeth and you most definitely need to shower. You still smell like smoke."

"Yeah, all right." Elliot moved to the single

kitchen drawer and pulled the first aid kit free. "But as soon as I'm done, I can't promise I'll keep my hands off you."

"I've been warned."

A few moments later, the door clicked softly, followed by the sound of water hitting tile as he disappeared into the bathroom. She picked up her lawyer's business card and Elliot's phone from the granite countertop. The zing of cold stone against her skin cleared her head of him. For now. What she wouldn't give to forget everything that'd happened the last few days, but without that chaos, she and Elliot would've kept up with their evasive dance. She would've come home from the lab every night, compete in the lyric trivia battle they'd created, drink his beer and go inside her apartment. Alone. Never knowing what it'd be like to kiss him, never knowing his touch, or what it'd feel like to have the kind of protection he offered. Never knowing love.

Inhaling deep, she fought to keep her head in the game. It wouldn't last long. Elliot Dunham had worked his way beneath her skin, down into her bones, and had become part of her. But she'd take advantage of the clarity to find the Genism employee who obviously wanted her dead. Dialing Blake Henson's number from his business card, she brought the phone to her ears.

Two rings. Three.

"Come on, pick up." Nervousness lodged in her throat. According to Alexis's corporate server his-

tory, someone in the legal department had orchestrated this entire puzzle. Blake Henson was the only resource they had to find their suspect. Without his willingness to hand over confidential documents identifying the subjects of her trials—the same subjects Alexis had compiled in her list—she and Elliot had nothing. She'd spend the rest of her life looking over her shoulder, paranoid about the next attack. She bounced on her toes as anxiety clawed up her throat. "Pick up the phone."

The line clicked. "Blake Henson."

Relief crashed through her. "Mr. Henson, it's Waylynn. Sorry, Dr. Hargraves. You know, the former employee currently under investigation for murdering my lab assistant."

"Doesn't ring a bell. I'm kidding, Dr. Hargraves. Of course I recognize your voice." A deep laugh reached through the line. "I was getting worried you wouldn't call, but I'm about to meet with the board of directors about your reinstatement. Can I call you back?"

"Actually, I wasn't calling about that. I need your help with something else." She dug the corner of his business card into her index finger. This had to work. There weren't any other options. "According to the Genism server history, my assistant was in the middle of compiling a list of subjects who volunteered for trials testing for the warrior gene. Each volunteer filled out a waiver before the trials began and was assigned a subject number to guard their privacy—"

"But you need the waivers to identify them to help clear your name of Ms. Jacobs's murder," Blake Henson said.

"Yes." Her throat threatened to close, and she gripped the business card harder. Would he help them, or would he report her request back to the board and terminate any chance she had of getting her job back? She didn't know him well enough to make a guess. He'd defended her during Anchorage PD's interrogation because it'd been his job—to protect Genism Corporation employees. But now that she wasn't an employee any longer... "I know what I'm asking you to do, but you're the only chance I have of finding who killed my assistant."

Seconds ticked by in silence, a full minute.

She checked the screen to ensure the call was still connected, but he hadn't hung up. Was he having the receptionist call the police as they spoke? Waylynn breathed through the pressure building behind her sternum. "Mr. Henson?"

"You said Ms. Jacobs was compiling a list of subjects who tested positive for the warrior gene. The only way she would've identified them was if someone from the legal department gave her the very same documents you're asking me to hand over." The lawyer's voice lowered to a whisper, and she had to remember he was about to meet with the board concerning her reinstatement. "Does that mean you think one of my colleagues is a murderer?"

The click of the bathroom door put her face-to-

face with a wall of muscle that threw her saliva glands into overdrive. The breath rushed out of her as the raw edges of his wound glimmered under the single lightbulb above the counter. Elliot carried fresh gauze and tape at his side but didn't move to repatch the bullet wound. She hit the button for speakerphone to bring him into the conversation. "I'm not sure, but anything you can provide may help the investigation."

"If I get you the documents you're asking for, I could lose my job. I could get sued by the lab, and believe me when I say they have a horde of bulldog attorneys I've worked with for years who will make sure I never practice law again." His hesitation slithered through her. One second. Two. "You'll have to meet me out of the city, away from Genism. Can you meet at Cliffside Marina in Whittier in two hours? Alone?"

Elliot shook his head slowly, a hint of that raging violence consuming his gaze. Gripping the towel around his hips, he accentuated the bruises and cuts along his white knuckles.

This was the only chance they had of uncovering what got Alexis Jacobs killed and why someone had framed her for it. Waylynn kept her focus on the man in front of her. "I'll be there."

"See you then." Blake Henson ended the call.

"What were you thinking agreeing to meet him alone?" Elliot asked.

"I was thinking it'd be nice if I didn't have to look

over my shoulder for the rest of my life, that I could end this nightmare, and move on." She set his phone back onto the counter, taking a deep breath. "I told you. Blake Henson isn't the man who drugged and framed me for Alexis's murder. He's taking a risk to help us."

"Someone is out to destroy you, and we've already proved your boss was involved, Doc. What makes you think whoever started this doesn't have someone else working for him?" Elliot ran a hand through his still-wet hair, shaking his head. The violence had cooled in his eyes, but tension tightened the muscles down his back as he turned away from her. "There's no way I'm letting you meet this guy by yourself."

"Here, let me help." She reached out for him, sliding her hand over his arm. Taking the gauze and tape from him, she crowded him until he sat on the bar stool. Someone had gone out of their way to destroy her and she wasn't stupid enough to meet her lawyer on her own. Didn't matter Elliot had lied about investigating her past or the fact he might pick up and leave Anchorage at the drop of a hat. She wanted him by her side. Forever. Because that was what love was. Compromising. Strong. Honest. The con man, the MIT drop out, the investigator, she loved them all. Waylynn cut a piece of gauze to size, then placed his hand over it while she ripped the last two pieces of tape from the roll to secure it in place.

He clamped a hand over hers as she pressed down the tape, running the pad of his thumb over the back of her hand. Her breath caught as he dragged her closer, the towel around his hips riding up his powerful thighs. Clean man and a hint of their burned breakfast from that morning filled her lungs, but every cell in her body stood at attention. For him. "Your safety is the only thing that matters to me, Doc. You're mine to protect. I failed once. It won't happen again."

"I know." But if her lawyer suspected she'd brought backup or that she'd been followed, he'd disappear with the files they needed to clear her name. Elliot's body heat beat against her and she finally looked up into those mesmerizing gray eyes. "What if I'm the only one Blake Henson sees? You'll be there, but in the background. Close enough to get to me if something goes wrong and we'll get what we need to identify the subjects Alexis was focused on."

"I'm calling in backup." He pushed to his feet, a corner of the gauze still free. "If the bastard comes at you again, we'll be ready."

"If that will make you feel better, then let's do it." Hell, having an entire team of trained professionals made *her* feel better. She slid her thumbnail around the empty roll of medical tape. "You ran out of tape, but I think I might have some in the first-aid kit I brought from my apartment."

He pulled her back into him by the hand, planting a hard rush-inducing kiss on her lips. "I'm going up to get dressed anyway and you still need to brush your teeth. I'll get it."

"All right. It should be in the bottom of my bag." Her fingers slipped from his as he headed upstairs. A smile played on her lips as he threw the towel over the balcony and she bit down on her thumbnail to keep herself in place. Together forever? That was a lot of horrible '90s country battles. Turning her attention back to the laptop and not to her imagination of him upstairs, she pulled more of her research off the servers as fast as she could before the IT department cut off her access. It was a miracle her login had worked this long. "Did you find the tape?"

Hardwood protested under his weight as Elliot came back down the stairs. "What the hell is this?"

Waylynn lifted her gaze, the smile disappearing. Her hand automatically clenched the edge of the granite countertop as she locked on her overnight bag in his hands and the gun she'd hidden in the bottom. No. No, no, no, no. She straightened, trying to control the panic exploding behind her sternum. "Elliot, listen to me, it's not what you think."

"Really?" He moved in on her, all predator and her the prey. "Because this looks a lot like the gun that was used to shoot your father fifteen years ago."

Chapter Twelve

Betrayal didn't start with big lies, but with small secrets.

And Waylynn holding on to the evidence in her father's murder investigation all these years was possibly one of the biggest betrayals he'd ever experienced. "Forget about the stash of cash and your passport. Why do you have the gun, Waylynn?"

Her mouth fell open. Ocean blue eyes snapped to the weapon. "You have to understand, I was fifteen. I was scared. I hid the gun thinking it would all go away. I knew it was wrong, but I thought if the police never found the murder weapon, they'd forget the whole thing."

The world fell out from under him. All this time, she'd kept evidence out of police custody, and a flood of fury burned through him. She'd spent the last four days trying to convince him she'd become the monster she'd feared, but he hadn't listened to any of it. Not her. Not the woman whose smile turned his entire day around. Not the woman who'd held her own in their private country competition. Not the woman he'd fallen in love with over the past ninety-six hours. He'd been wrong. Elliot pointed one finger at her, the weapon tight in his hand. "You lied to me."

"No. I never lied to you." She moved forward, but he countered her advance. Her expression fell as she slowed a few feet from him. "I just didn't tell you the whole truth."

"Then tell me the truth now." Whom the hell had he been protecting? Whom had he taken a bullet for back at the crash site? All this time she'd played the victim, manipulating him to believe her innocence. Had he been staring at—making love to—a murderer instead? Bile pushed into his throat. He'd done a lot of bad stuff in his life, but he'd drawn the line at murder. And Waylynn… "Did you kill your father?"

She picked at her chipped nails, her throat working to swallow. Her shoulder rose on a deep inhale and she dropped her hands to her sides, her mind made up by the sternness in her expression. "I can't tell you that. Because if I do, you won't see me as a friend anymore…as a partner. I need you to trust me."

"Can't? Or won't?" He turned his back to her, the gun still in his hand. How had he not seen it before? He'd read the police report of that night. Police hadn't been able to recover the murder weapon and he'd chalked it up to human error. Evidence went missing all the time in high-profile cases like Nathan Hargraves's. In reality, the truth crushed the air from his lungs. "I just found a gun from a fifteen-year-old murder in your bag. Any trust you earned with me is gone."

"Please." She reached out for him, but suddenly thought better of it. "Elliot, I wish I could—"

"Could what?" Twisting around, he struggled to contain the rage exploding through him. "Take it all back? Tell me the truth from the beginning? I put my life on the line, took a bullet and nearly died in a fire for you. Because I believed you were innocent." Pain set up residence behind his sternum. She'd played him, manipulated him. Used him. Just as his parents and the Iraqi guards had with their head games and steel bars. "You're just as guilty as the bastard targeting you, aren't you? You killed your father and hid the evidence to avoid prosecution. I guess you were right before, Waylynn. You are a monster."

He regretted the words the moment they left his mouth, but the damage had already been done. No matter how much his instincts protested that statement, she'd killed a man in cold blood and kept the evidence hidden.

And he couldn't love her.

Waylynn blinked as though shock had punched her straight in the stomach and shot her hand out toward the counter for balance. Swiping her tongue across her bottom lip, she nodded, but refused to look at him. Shame. Guilt. Reality closed in on her features, and his gut clenched. In an instant, the grief had passed, control crossing her expression as she nailed him with her cold gaze. "What about the lies you've told, Elliot? What about the people you've hurt or the money you've stolen?" She pulled the storage device from his laptop and held it up. "What about the fact you swore to me you've never investigated my background, but have my father's police report on this thumb drive?"

"You're comparing my job protecting you to homicide?" He shouldn't have lied about the investigation into her past, but he'd told her the truth. There was no file on her. He hadn't started gathering information to use against her like he had the others. He hadn't had any intention of ever blackmailing her down the line. He'd requested the report from Vincent to make sure what was happening now wasn't tied to her past. That was his job. The second they'd tied Genism to Alexis's murder, he'd pulled the file into the trash. Only he hadn't realized there was a copy left on the thumb drive. Elliot set the gun on the counter, leaving it wrapped in the old T-shirt—the one spotted with blood—to preserve any fingerprints it might've held on to over the last fifteen years. It took every ounce of energy not to sink to the floor as his heart tore itself to pieces. "I'm only going to ask you one more time and I want an answer. Did you kill Nathan Hargraves?"

"I think you already have the answer you want. I'm a monster, remember?" Anger hollowed her voice, but she'd had to have known this day would come. Ripping her overnight bag from his grasp, she tucked it under her arm and headed for the front door. Hand on the dead bolt, she slowed. "Are you going to turn the gun in to the police?"

The bullet wound in his shoulder burned with renewed vigor. The last four days—aside from getting tasered, shot and nearly roasted to death—had been the best in his life. She'd given him a glimpse of real happiness. Given him a glimpse of the future. One where he didn't have to worry about the debt hanging over his head, putting his life on the line every day for people he didn't know, or looking over his shoulder the rest of his life for victims of his past. There was only her. And she was going to throw that all away. Blackhawk Security operatives protected those who couldn't protect themselves, by any means necessary. They broke laws, avoided authorities, kept their clients alive at the cost of their own lives. They hunted murderers. They didn't become them and they sure as hell didn't protect them. "Yes."

She nodded but refused to look back at him. She wrenched the door open. "I trusted you, too, Elliot. Remember that when you realize the mistake you've made, but don't you dare come looking for me. I don't *ever* want to see you again."

The cabin windows shook as she slammed the door behind her.

He should go after her. They were in the middle of the woods, for crying out loud. Chances of her getting lost, running into Mabel and her calves or something far worse happening increased with every step she took outside the perimeter of the cabin. But he couldn't force himself to move. He stretched the fingers of his uninjured hand, only now realizing he'd drawn blood with his nails. Pressure built in his head the longer he stared after her. He didn't protect killers and that was exactly what she was. A cold-blooded killer.

"Son of a bitch." She shouldn't be out there on her own. She'd betrayed him, manipulated him, but he didn't want to find the woman dead in the morning. The sun had met the horizon, darkness was closing in. Elliot scooped his phone, the gun and keys from the countertop and hit the speed dial for Blackhawk's forensics expert on his way to the front door. Two rings. Three. He exhaled hard as Vincent Kalani's voice mail filled the line. "I promise to stop stealing your lunch from the office fridge if you call me back in the next two minutes. No promises after that."

He hung up. Falling snow melted against his exposed skin as he wrenched open the SUV's driver's side door and climbed behind the wheel. Tossing his phone into the passenger seat, he engaged the headlights. Hell, he hated the snow. Pulling a flashlight from the supplies stashed under the back seat, he scanned the clearing around the cabin. Nothing but thick trees stared back at him as his boots hit the ground and he headed deeper into the forest. The headlights helped, but not much. "Waylynn!"

No answer.

Footprints imprinted in the dirt at the bottom of the cabin steps. Hell if he knew the plan when he found her. Turn her over to his team at Blackhawk Security? Drive her directly into Anchorage PD custody? He had to find her first. He'd worry about the plan later. Elliot brushed aside low-hanging branches, dry foliage and twigs crunching beneath his weight. He followed her shallow footprints. "Come on, Doc. Where are you?"

She couldn't have gotten that far on foot. Not in the dark. The road they'd driven up was the only clear path to the main highway, but sooner than he expected, her footprints disappeared. The ground was too dry here. Slowing, he held his breath to listen for any sign of movement, any sign she was close by. An owl hooted above him, kicking his nerves into high alert. "Waylynn!"

Running a hand through his hair, he dislodged snowflakes and wiped his hand down his jeans. Tendrils of their conversation—of him finding the gun—played through his head on repeat. No. The only reason he'd come out here was to make sure she paid for what she'd done. Nothing more. Elliot swung the flashlight into the tree line on either side of the road. No sign of her. He exhaled hard, dropping the flashlight to his side. His senses adjusted slowly to the dark, but it didn't make a damn bit of difference.

He was too late.

She'd disappeared.

YOU ARE A MONSTER.

Waylynn swiped at her face for the millionth time as she pushed through thick wilderness and dead leaves. Branches scraped at her skin, drawing blood, but she couldn't stop. Couldn't go back. Hadn't she gone far enough to reach the main road?

Exhaustion claimed her muscles as she'd practically run from the cabin—from him—but she hadn't had any other choice. He was going to turn over the gun used to kill her father to the police. She locked her teeth against the truth. He was going to turn *her* over. Her side of the story wouldn't matter. Not when it came to homicide. Even fifteen years later. The statute of limitations would never run out.

She had money. Her passport was still valid. She could run. She'd stored the thumb drive with her research into her bag. There were plenty of labs around the country who'd be willing to take her on. She'd be cleared of Alexis's murder. Officer Ramsey had all but indicated she was before Waylynn had left the scene of the fire at Genism.

Instead, she slowed her pace as dead silence and blackness surrounded her. A short burst of laughter escaped up her throat. Whom was she kidding? Unless she changed her name—started a whole new life—Elliot would find her. That was his job. Hugging her bag closer, she leaned against a large tree for support. She struggled to catch her breath and checked over her shoulder. Only hints of sunlight reached this far into the forest. She'd stuck to the road leading to his cabin for a few hundred feet but trailed off as she'd heard him call her name. No. He didn't get to come after her, didn't get to apologize.

He didn't get to play the hero this time.

"Come on, Hargraves. You've got to move." Blinking back the haze of anger, she forced one foot in front of the other. She couldn't stay out here all night. Snow had started falling again, temperatures dropping even in the middle of summer. Elliot had unloaded the tiny cabin close to the mountain range and if she got stuck out here for another hour, she'd freeze to death. And she just couldn't give him the satisfaction.

Frigid wind slammed into her, cutting through the light sweatshirt she'd brought with her. Straight down into bone, but she pushed on. Where was the damn highway? Her teeth chattered as a thousand different emotions bubbled inside her. Fury, confusion, hurt. A sharp ache expanded from behind her sternum. Or was it from the invisible knife he'd stabbed into her back? She'd protected herself—kept herself from opening up to anyone—for the past fifteen years, but Elliot Dunham had shoved her from one end of the emotional gauntlet to the other in seconds. Mere hours ago, she'd been wrapped in his arms, whispering promises, making plans. He'd made her believe they could be happy, that he didn't care about the darkness ingrained in her genetic code.

Then he'd destroyed it all. He'd confirmed the fear she'd carried with her since taking her very first blood test in Genism's warrior gene trial, the trial based off her research.

She'd let him in. And he'd betrayed her.

How could she have been so stupid? A growl escaped from between her lips, embarrassment heating her from the inside, but it wasn't enough to make a difference in her frozen fingers or numb toes. She shook her head and tried to bundle deeper into her sweatshirt. Maybe if she kept thinking of all the stupid decisions she'd made over the last four days—how she'd actually believed he could love her—she'd generate enough body heat to keep her alive out here.

"Where is the damn road?" Waylynn slowed again, listening for any sign she was headed in the right direction. Elliot hadn't driven more than twenty minutes off the main highway. She'd covered at least a mile on foot, what she could feel of her feet aching in the thin shoes offering no support. What exactly was her plan once she reached the road? Flag down a vehicle? Hitchhike to the meeting with her former lawyer at the marina? Chances of finding someone going straight there were slim. She deflated on the spot, knees weak, exhausted. And her heart... She rubbed at her chest as a fresh wave of tears burned in her eyes. Her heart was tired, damn it.

White light moved over her, and she raised her hands to block the beams. The air rushed from her lungs. Headlights. The sound of tires on road grew louder, then softer within a beat of her pulse. Shoving to her feet, Waylynn ignored the pain and followed the retreating vehicle until her shoes hit solid ground. A burst of relieved laughter escaped her throat. She'd made it and another car was approaching.

"Hey!" She stepped out a few feet into the road, swinging her arm overhead. The car arched away from her, didn't stop. Two more cars passed, neither pulling over. She couldn't miss the meeting with Blake Henson. Everything—finding Alexis's murderer, avoiding a murder in the first-degree charge, getting her job back—depended on it. She should've stolen Elliot's keys and taken the SUV, but she'd had to put as much distance between them as possible. Walking backward, Waylynn stuck out her thumb as another vehicle approached. "Please pull over. Please."

The car drove straight past her.

"You've got to be kidding me. Really? Is there no such thing as human decency left in this city!" Dropping her hand, she kicked hard at a loose rock on the shoulder. Clouds turned violet, blue and orange as the sun continued its slow crawl across the horizon, barely making the road in front of her visible. Screeching tires filled her ears and she snapped her head up. The sleek black car had stopped in the middle of the road. Waited. For her? Exhaust and a hint of gasoline filled her lungs as she took a single step toward the vehicle. The hairs raised on the back of her neck, her scalp pulling tight in warning. That car was the only one that'd stopped, was her only shot of getting out of here and to her meeting, but no matter how hard she pushed for her feet to move, they wouldn't obey.

No. Something wasn't right about this.

Red taillights highlighted asphalt as the driver put the car in Reverse and her instincts kicked into a nervous overdrive. She twisted around, headed in the opposite direction. Shoving her hands into her pockets, she held her bag close to her ribs. She should've grabbed the gun before running into the woods. She scanned the road in front of her. Twigs. Small rocks. Nothing that could really be used to protect herself. Air froze in her lungs as the car reentered her peripheral vision driving backward down a seventy-mile-an-hour highway.

The passenger side window slid down, the outline of the driver clear, but she refused to look up. Another car sped past, but she caught the driver's question above the noise of tires and road. "Need a ride?"

"No, thank you." Waylynn pushed the pain in her feet to the back of her mind. She had to keep walking. Sweat beaded at her temple despite the dropping temperatures. "I'm fine."

Shoving the vehicle into Park, the driver hit the pavement, one arm draped over the roof. "Come on now, Dr. Hargraves. Get in. At least let me get you to the meeting with your lawyer."

She stopped cold. Puffs of crystallized air formed in front of her lips, every muscle in her body strung tight. She raised her gaze, only the shadowy outline of the driver visible. Male. Tall. At least six feet.

Wearing a baseball cap. No facial features she could make out. Nothing to suggest she'd met this man before. "How do you know my name?"

How did he know about the meeting with her lawyer?

"I know everything about you, Waylynn." He slammed the door closed and rounded in front of the headlights. The falling snow, coupled with the fact he was too tall for the headlights to identify him, pooled dread at the base of her spine. But it was the gun in his hand that claimed most of her attention. "And the best thing you can do for yourself is get in the car."

Waylynn ditched her bag and ran like the devil. Broken branches and vines threatened to trip her as she headed for the trees. She wouldn't look back. Wouldn't see if the driver had followed her. Wouldn't give up that easily. She was a survivor and she'd fight like hell to stay that way. Her lungs burned with shallow breaths, but she didn't slow. Because the crunching sound of dead foliage and twigs behind her meant he'd come after her. Pain pulled at her, slowed her down. No. This wasn't how she was going to die.

Two gunshots exploded in her ears and she wrapped her hands around the back of her head in an attempt to protect herself from a bullet. Pain erupted through her left arm instead and she screamed as her nerve endings caught fire. She plowed into a tree shoulder-first as the initial shock took hold, momentum spinning her toward the shooter. Her flimsy shoe caught on a root climbing from the earth and she fell back. Dead leaves and dirt worked into her eyes and mouth as she rolled down the small incline. Waylynn shot her hand out to grab something—anything—to keep her from falling and latched on to a loose root.

The world fought to right itself as the dizziness fled. She pulled at the root with her uninjured arm, but adrenaline could push her only so far. She was exhausted, bleeding. Her ears rang, but through the high-pitched keen, she picked up the sound of rushing water. A river. Looking down at her feet, she suppressed the scream working up her throat at the sight of how close she'd come to death. She struggled for purchase no more than twelve inches from the edge of a small cliff that ended in a raging river below. She couldn't breathe, couldn't think, her hand gripped tight around the root. If the madman who'd shot her in the middle of the damn wilderness didn't kill her, the river would. Waylynn tugged at the root again, but it gave way. Another scream escaped as reality set in. No one could help her now.

A rough hand clamped onto her arm a split second before she plunged into the violent waters below, a hand with a raised scar across the back. "Oh, no, Dr. Hargraves. I'm not finished with you yet."

Chapter Thirteen

You are a monster. Had he really thrown that in her face? The constant replay of their conversation echoed in his head as he hiked through another trail leading toward the main road. It was stupid to give in to the guilt eating him alive from the inside when he finally understood what she was, but the emotion proved too strong to fight. He'd used her one fear against her and now she was missing. Damn it. As far as he could tell, she'd headed straight into the woods to lose him.

Three sets of headlights illuminated the trees and brush around him. He tapped the earpiece he kept on hand to connect to the rest of the team when they came into range and stepped out into the small dirt road leading up to the cabin. Vincent, Elizabeth, Sullivan and Anthony all hit the dirt at the same time and surveyed their surroundings. Just as they'd been trained. "Hey, look. It's the strippers I ordered."

"You can't afford me." Sullivan Bishop took the phone Vincent offered him, swiping his thumb over the screen, and held it up. He turned in a wide circle. The former Navy SEAL had come strapped and ready for war. They all had. "How long has she been on foot?"

Elliot strangled the guilt and rage. He never should've let her walk out that door, but neither did him a damn bit of good right now. Now all he could do was find her. "An hour. She headed down the road for about two hundred feet, then veered north, straight into the woods. I've searched four grids, all around the spot she took cover in the trees. No sign of her."

"We're out of range." Elizabeth stuffed her own phone into her pocket. "There's no way she would've been able to call someone for a ride. She has to still be out there."

Not only were they out of range, but he'd also ditched her phone when he'd determined it was tapped, right before the car accident. No. She couldn't call anyone. Couldn't ask for help.

"By 'took cover' you mean went into hiding?" Sullivan asked. "What the hell happened, Dunham? Last time I checked, that woman wouldn't leave your side."

Elliot ran his uninjured hand through his hair. What'd happened? He'd screwed up. That was what had happened. There were at least a dozen other ways he could've approached the subject of the gun, but instead, he'd taken her betrayal personally. Searching for her a quarter mile in every direction, clearing her crimes, she didn't deserve to be hunted like an animal for the rest of her life. He closed in on Kate's SUV as the former psychologist climbed out of the driver's seat.

And slowed.

Where grief normally shadowed the blonde's expression, the hopelessness in her gaze pierced him straight to the core. "Something's happened."

"I'm sorry, Elliot. I pulled over on the side of the highway at the road entrance to see if she'd made it that far." The team converged on their profiler as Kate reached into the SUV, her focus entirely on him. She slammed her door closed, holding a medium-sized brightly colored bag at her side. "And I found this."

Waylynn's bag.

A high-pitched ringing filled his ears, a cold sweat shooting down his back. He forced himself to reach for the bag and curled his fingers in the faux tanned leather. The weight pulled at him and he didn't have to look inside to know it was still full of her clothing and toiletries. "Where?"

Kate crossed her arms and leaned her weight against the SUV, her voice hollow. Platinum blonde hair escaped the tight bun at the back of her neck as she pulled her phone from her signature green cargo jacket, her husband's. She offered him the device. "About thirty yards from the road. I took a picture before moving it. Looked like she'd ditched it in a his head, worried he'd find her body out here, he'd realized she hadn't kept her father's murder weapon to hurt him. She'd kept it to protect herself. Physically or from a murder charge, he had no idea. Didn't change the fact he'd trusted her, believed her innocence, had slept with her, but he never should've judged her for how she'd chosen to survive. As she'd rightly pointed out, he'd done things—hurt people— to do the same. Waylynn was gone, but he sure as hell wouldn't give up on finding her. "All that matters is that we find her."

Wrenching his SUV driver's side door open, he gripped the gun Waylynn had left behind and handed it to Vincent with the old T-shirt still wrapped around the handle. No more lies. No more secrets. The forensics expert would tell him who killed Nathan Hargraves and then he would get back out there and search this entire state if he had to, to find her. "I need you to run prints on this as soon as possible."

And if they came back as Waylynn's... He'd figure it out after he found her.

"All right. I'll do it." Vincent Kalani towered over him, a Hawaiian giant with tattoos up and down his neck and curly, black hair that extended to the middle of his back. Unfolding his arms, the former cop pointed a single finger at him with one hand and took the gun with the other. "But only if you swear to stop stealing my food."

He'd do whatever he had to, to get to the truth. His future depended on it. "Deal."

hurry. I had to recollect some of the items that'd fallen out. Including this."

Blackhawk's profiler handed him an all-too-familiar storage drive.

The one Waylynn had used to save her research.

Elliot tightened his grip on the phone. Kate was right. From the looks of it, Waylynn had obviously ditched the bag in a hurry, but she never would've left her research behind. Which meant... "He has her."

"What's the profile say, Kate? We've got to find this bastard before someone else gets hurt." Sullivan took the phone before Elliot could crush it in his hand and studied the photo.

Elliot didn't hear a damn word. Forget the investigation. Forget the profile. Forget Vincent's report. The SOB who'd framed Waylynn for murder had reached the end of his rope. He was going to kill her. Racing for the SUV, he ignored the pain shooting through his shoulder and ripped open the driver's-side door. He tossed her bag in the back seat and shoved the keys into the ignition.

"Elliot, you're not going to find him on your own." Elizabeth Dawson planted her palms on the hood of the vehicle, short dark hair swinging forward from behind her cars. "We're a team. You need us."

"You're not going to want me on your team after you see what I do to him." The words growled from his throat. He revved the engine. He'd never hurt Liz, but he had no problem making her think he would to get to Waylynn. She was the only one who mattered. She was…everything. And he loved her. Didn't matter if she'd killed her father. Didn't matter she'd hidden the evidence for the last fifteen years. Or if she'd turn into someone he didn't recognize years down the road from some genetic marker. She was his. And he had to get to her. Now.

"Probably." Elizabeth held up her phone, the Genism logo clear in the upper left-hand corner of the screen. "But I'm the one who knows how to find her."

He put the SUV in Park and got out. "What is that?"

"I was able to save a chunk of data to my computer from the hard drive before it was stolen. Braxton's been working on it since the break-in. Says he's going to kill the guy himself if he finds him." Elizabeth offered him the phone. "He recovered a readable copy of the list Alexis Jacobs was building from the genetics trials and just sent it to me. Names and everything."

Elliot ran his finger down the side of the screen. Adrenaline sharpened his senses, hiked his blood pressure rate higher. They had a lead. If one of the people on this list put their hands on Waylynn… He focused on one name in particular, reading it three times before the puzzle pieces fell into place, and let the violence boiling inside him take control. "I know where he took her, and I know who he is."

A HIGH-PITCHED WHIRLING sound pulled her from unconsciousness.

Waylynn swallowed around the horrible taste in

her mouth. Dirt and…salt? Straightening her neck, she oriented herself and blinked to clear the haze. Her shirt had plastered to her skin, soaked. With blood. Where was she? Movement registered a few feet away from her and she tensed. But couldn't move. Panic exploded through her and she pulled at her wrists as the flood of her last moments before her attacker injected her with a syringe rushed forward. She shut her eyes tight to work through the burst of pain in her arm. How could she have forgotten she'd been shot? "You shot me."

A wave of dizziness pitched her stomach into nauseous territory. Or had the white stuccoed surface beneath her actually moved?

"I've seen what you're capable of, Dr. Hargraves, remember?" Her lawyer, Blake Henson, crouched in front of her, a drill in his scarred left hand. The opposite hand he'd used to give her his business card back at the lab. Fear climbed up her spine, tightening the muscles down her spine. It was him. Blake Henson killed her assistant. Drugged her. Framed her for murder. Impossibly blue eyes steadied on her as she fought the churn of nausea working up her throat. "I couldn't take any chances."

"In that case, I have a problem with the customer service here. Can I speak to the manager?" She forced herself to look past him, to the steering wheel and small windshield, the padded seats, the clean, tan-and-navy color scheme. Salt and humidity dived into her lungs. They were on a boat. Maybe at the marina where she was supposed to meet him. Only now she understood. He'd never intended to hand over those documents and help clear her name. He'd set all of this up from the beginning. But none of that explained the drill in his hand. Didn't matter. She wasn't going to hang around long enough for him to use it. Stretching her fingers behind her, she brushed against the seat at her back but didn't feel anything that could be used to free herself. "You killed Alexis. Destroyed my research. Framed me. What did I ever do to you?"

"Yes, well, I had to make it look like you'd do anything to protect your precious warrior gene trials after I killed Alexis." Henson slipped his index finger over the trigger of the drill. "Shame, too. I was actually starting to think she and I had a future together. I was going to propose." His expression hardened in the dim light coming off the horizon. "Then she started compiling a list of Genism employees and consultants who tested positive for the warrior gene, my name included. When my firm had first been put on retainer, we were asked to provide a blood sample by the board of directors. Genism policy. Once she confirmed I carried the variant, too, she'd started pulling away. Wouldn't return my calls." Her lawyer gripped the drill so hard in his apparent anger, he didn't notice the extra drill bit magnetized to the base of the tool had slipped to the boat's deck. "She was going to go to the board, cost me everything I'd worked for the last fifteen years. She was going to leave me. And I couldn't have that."

Waylynn positioned her foot over the slim piece of steel. It wasn't much as a weapon, but it was something. Maybe enough to cut the plastic around her wrists. She just had to keep him talking. "And somehow you learned about my past."

"Your previous murder accusation did come in handy." Anger consumed his expression, a glint that was dark and violent and utterly menacing, but she'd seen scary. And this man? He didn't have Elliot's smile. "Who better to pin your assistant's death on than a woman who's already shown she's capable of murder?"

Her heart panged at the simple thought of Elliot's name, but she bit back the urge to react. She had to stay in control. She had to get out of this. Because he wasn't coming to save her this time. Pulling her foot inward, she maneuvered the drill bit that much closer toward her hand. She didn't bother denying her lawyer's allegation. The courts had brought the charges against her fifteen years ago despite the truth and he wouldn't give a damn about what'd really happened. A few more inches. That was all she needed. "And Matt? What did he have to do with any of this?"

"A tool. Nothing more." Blake Henson stood, his knees popping as he straightened. Two steps. Three. He placed the drill above a large, clear, plastic box she hadn't noticed until now and compressed the trigger. The high-pitched whirling started again as pressure built in her chest.

Waylynn dug her heels into the deck. Oh, no. No, no, no, no. This wasn't happening. Darkness closed in around the edges of her vision, her breath coming in short bursts. Pulling at the zip ties again, she locked her jaw against the scream working up her throat. She wasn't going in that box. Stretching to reach the drill bit sticking out from beneath the heel of her shoe, she cut the edge of her finger.

The sound of the drill died as Blake Henson pulled the steel bit from the box. "Alexis showed me the list she built identifying subjects who carried your little warrior gene. Of course, I was surprised to find you on the list, Doctor. Didn't think you had it in you. No pun intended." His short burst of laughter only solidified the dread pooling at the base of her spine. "From there it wasn't hard to aim Matt Stover in your direction. He felt lied to, manipulated, believed you'd destroy everything you and he had built for Genism for your own gain. Of course, some of those ideas might not have been his own. I gave him the idea to start tracking your phone, to wait for the perfect opportunity to strike when you were released from police custody."

"Why defend me at all?" she asked. "Why not let the police charge me with murder? You said you were my lawyer!"

"I wouldn't be playing my part if I hadn't shown up in my legal capacity. It would have been conspicuous by my absence." A furrow appeared between his eyebrows, as though his answer hadn't been obvious. "I needed you close. I needed you to not suspect I was the one who'd killed Alexis in case your memory returned. The cocktail I dosed you with that night is powerful, but not always reliable."

"So many bodies." But she wouldn't be one of them. Waylynn palmed the drill bit and worked at the zip tie behind her back. No. She'd fight because she'd had to her entire life. She didn't know how to die quietly. Was the drill bit cutting through the plastic? She had no idea, but she wasn't going to sit here and let Blake Henson decide what to do with her. And she was done being his puppet. "You're a psychopath."

"I prefer *creative*." He set the drill down on the driver's seat and hefted the lid off the box. "Like it? I'd like to say I came up with the idea all by myself, but your colleagues were really the ones who gave me the idea. You see, this plastic is near unbreakable. It can keep a number of contaminants from escaping the lab, only I've made a few adjustments to suit my needs."

She was running out of time. The drill bit hadn't cut through the zip ties as fast as she thought it would and Blake Henson's tone suggested he'd started winding down. "What did you drug me with that night? Why couldn't the toxicology report find anything after the police took my blood?"

"You're stalling, Dr. Hargraves." Her lawyer laid

the lid to the box—her intended coffin—against the side of the boat. In her next breath, he stood over her. "Whatever you're planning, it won't work. I made the mistake of trying to come at you indirectly twice now, but I've learned my lesson."

Desperation clawed through her. Time had run out. Waylynn tugged at the zip ties. "You don't have to do this. Just because you're a carrier for the warrior gene doesn't mean the board will let you go. I can help you. I can—"

"I'm not interested in your help, Doctor. You've already cost me everything I cared about." Gripping her arms, Blake Henson ripped her from the deck. The boat swayed, forcing her into him. He tugged her toward the clear box, the one he'd drilled holes into. "And now it's your turn."

"All this talking is giving me a headache." Trying to wrench out of his hold, she aggravated the bullet wound in her arm and nearly lost consciousness from the agony tearing through her. How could Elliot still stand after taking a bullet in the shoulder? Her flimsy shoes slipped on the boat's deck, but he only held her tighter. He was so much stronger, so much bigger, but she kept fighting. She'd die in that box if she gave up now. "No!"

The zip ties snapped. Swinging the drill bit as hard as she could, she planted it straight into his arm, in almost exactly the same location he'd shot her. His roar threatened to burst her eardrums a split second before the back of his hand met her face. Waylynn hit the deck. Hard. Temporary blackness clouded her vision, but she pushed to her feet. Couldn't stop. Pain lightninged through her arm, threatening to undo her, as she lunged for the back of the boat. "Help!"

A bloodied hand wrapped around her mouth and pulled her into her attacker's chest. Blake Henson's mouth pressed against her ear. "You're going to pay for that."

She wrenched her elbow back as hard as she could but lost momentum as he hefted her off her feet. The boat, the marina, everything blurred as her lawyer tossed her over his shoulder in a fireman's carry. Kicking, punching, she battled to get free with every last ounce of strength.

It wasn't enough.

Dumping her into the plastic box he'd prepared, Henson knocked the air from her lungs, momentarily paralyzing her long enough to get the lid in place.

"No! No!" She pounded on the plastic, each hit reverberating through the box. Kicking at the bottom of the container, Waylynn struggled to lift her knees up enough to gain leverage. There wasn't any room. Small holes provided enough oxygen, but she'd never felt so claustrophobic in her life. He'd sealed her inside her own coffin. She set her palms against the lid as tears streaked down her face into her hairline. "Please. Don't do this."

"The holes I've drilled into the bottom of the box are small enough to ensure you don't die too quickly. Wouldn't want you not to suffer, now would we?"

Blake Henson watched her struggle from above. Anchoring his hands on either side of the plastic container, he bent over her. Face-to-face with two inches of biocontainment plastic between them. "Don't worry, Dr. Hargraves. Genism will be fine without you."

Without another word, her lawyer straightened, then hauled her and the box toward the back of the boat. Her throat stung from screaming, her knuckles bled from hitting the lid with everything she had left. No. This wasn't how she wanted to die. Her attacker slid the bottom of the box out the back of the boat, nothing but a sea of black below.

A flashlight beam caught her attention through the plastic.

"Waylynn!" Elliot pumped his legs hard across the dock and she pressed her hands against the lid in an effort to reach out for him.

Right as Blake Henson dropped her into the ocean.

Chapter Fourteen

She was in the water.

Bullets ripped past his head as Blake Henson balanced on the back of his boat, but Elliot had only one focus.

"Waylynn!" His lungs struggled to keep up with the rest of his body as he hurdled over a coil of rope toward the spot he'd seen her go in. If anything happened to her, the bastard would pay, but he couldn't go after the lawyer now. Gunfire erupted from the docks and forced Henson to take cover. Elliot's team had his back and it would have to be enough for now. He tossed the flashlight. One step. Two. He launched himself off the end of the dock.

Freezing water shocked every nerve ending he owned as he hit the water, but it wasn't enough to stop him from diving deeper. Bubbles and darkness made it nearly impossible to see through the water. His ears popped as he sank lower, pressure building in his lungs. He couldn't see her. Stretching out his hands, he grazed something hard and latched on to the smooth edges of what felt like a large aquatic box for swimming with sharks. His senses adjusted slowly, murky water and seaweed clearing just enough—enough to see her terrified expression through the container Henson had sealed her in.

She beat against the lid wildly. Bubbles escaped the small holes down by her feet, the water level slowly rising inside the clear coffin. She was going to drown. Elliot slid his fingers around the edge of the box, ignoring the rush of pain in his shoulder. How the hell had her kidnapper sealed this thing? His heartbeat pounded loud behind his ears as the frigid temperature slowed his movements. Low thumps reverberated through him, bullets from the battle above slicing through the water around them. The water level had reached her knees as the weight of the box pulled her deeper into the ocean.

They were running out of time.

Gripping the edges of the box, he tried hauling it toward the surface. In vain. The damn thing was too heavy, and his muscles had lost strength due to his wound. Elliot tapped on the glass to get her attention and pointed to the ocean floor. He'd swim down to find something—a rock, a stray piece of metal, anything—to pry the container open. Her palms flattened against the clear plastic as he swam deeper into the gloom below them. Tons of water threatened to crush him as he reached the sandy bottom of the marina. Skimming his hand along the surface, he gripped a sharp rock and headed straight back up to where he thought her last position to be.

She wasn't there. Waylynn and the box had shifted with the undertow.

His lungs ached. His body had burned through his oxygen supply faster than he'd estimated. Catching sight of her outline as she sank farther into the depths, Elliot had to make a choice. Surface for air and risk getting shot in the process. Or lose consciousness trying to get her out now. Every instinct protested leaving her down here alone, but he had to surface. Rock in hand, he struggled topside. His clothing pulled at him, his boots heavy.

A bright wave of fire consumed the surface as a blast knocked him off course.

Elliot curled in on himself and pushed away from the surface as debris hit the water from an explosion above. An entire leather seat crashed directly above him, but he couldn't kick fast enough to avoid the collision. Metal tore into his thigh, ripping through his jeans, skin and into the muscle. A garbled scream pulled reserved air from his lungs as he clamped a hand down on the wound. The debris had missed major arteries, but he wasn't sure how much time he had left before he passed out from blood loss. He couldn't hold his breath any longer. Every second he wasted cost Waylynn valuable time and the more he bled, the more predators would start hunting. He pushed to the surface and gasped for oxygen. Pain burned through him with each kick. "Holy hell, that hurts."

"Over here!" Kate screamed over her shoulder from the dock and reached for him. "Give me your hand. I'll pull you out."

"She's stuck down there, Kate, and I can't get her out. I'm not going anywhere." He sucked down air as fast as he could, trying to expand his lungs for another chance. She was alone. She was scared. Heat seared along his face and neck. Pieces of burning wood floated around him. "Find me a tool. A crowbar. Anything that can break through thick plastic."

"Kate! Gear up!" Footsteps sounded on the dock behind her. Vincent appeared at her side, hauling an oxygen tank from his shoulder and dropping scuba gear to the dock. Blackhawk's forensics expert pounded the end of a flare against the pier, bright white magnesium lighting a marina already on fire, then tossed it into the ocean. The red glow flickered as the flare sank. He sparked another and threw it down. "These should help."

"Where's Henson?" he asked.

"Elliot, get down there." Kate ripped her husband's jacket off and stripped out of her shirt. Medium-length, flowing blond hair skimmed her sports bra as she pushed her jeans down her legs. "I'll be ready in fifteen seconds. Go!"

He'd have to ask about the explosion later. After he got Waylynn out of that damn box. Elliot dived. Swimming with every last ounce of strength he had left, he followed the trail of small bubbles coming from the blackness below, lit by Vincent's flares. She still had oxygen. How much, he had no idea, but it wouldn't last forever. Tendrils of blood seeped from both wounds and wove in front of his face, but he only pushed harder. She might've given up on him, but he wouldn't leave her to die.

The light from the flares reflected off a solid surface below. Waylynn. The panic in her ocean-blue gaze cut through him as he gripped onto the edges of the box again. The undertow pulled to rip him away, but he only held tighter. He wouldn't fail her again. Not this intelligent, mind-blowing, sexy creature who'd crashed into his existence and defied everything he'd known about what real happiness was. The box had leveled out along the sandy floor, submerging her in water from head to toe. Water lapped at the edges of her temples as she screamed, dark mascara running down her face.

A gloved hand slipped over his shoulder and he spun to find Kate in full scuba gear beside him. She pulled her mouthpiece free and handed it to him. Exhaling the air he'd been coveting, he maneuvered the rubber into his mouth and inhaled deep. A burst of cold oxygen filled his lungs and he handed the mouthpiece back. The tank had enough oxygen to last the two of them for at least another thirty minutes, but Waylynn...

She wouldn't last much longer.

A sharp pain lanced through him. That wasn't

an option. He needed her. He wasn't sure how much until this very moment, but there was no denying it now.

He wedged his hands on either side of the box and kicked with everything he had. The lid didn't budge. The bubbles escaping through the two small holes in the bottom of the container tickled along his skin and face. They had to stop the intake of water. Tapping on Kate's shoulder, he pointed to them. She nodded, swimming behind him and plugging them with her gloves as much as she could. It wasn't a permanent fix, but it'd give Waylynn more time. The water lapped at her mouth and nose as she pressed against the lid of the box. He searched the marina floor, this time in the light of two flares still burning bright a few yards away. Magnesium burned hot enough to melt through the thickest metal. Plastic shouldn't hold one of those flares back. But he could hit Waylynn's skin in the process.

His movements slowed as the frigid temperature cut through his clothing, past skin, past muscle and straight into his bones. He was losing blood with every pump of his legs as he closed in on the nearest flare. Careful not to stare at the magnesium fire directly, he grabbed what was left of the casing and swam as fast as he could to Waylynn.

They were going to get her out. Because if they didn't… He'd go back to prison. Nobody would be able to stop him from tearing Blake Henson apart with his bare hands.

He moved the flare over the lid, shocked to find a wide, dark stain blooming across her white shirt he hadn't noticed before. Blood. Rage threatened to consume him. What the hell had that bastard done to her? Elliot forced himself to focus, forced himself to ignore the haze of red spreading across his vision. One second. Two. Putting the flare to the plastic would get the job done, but there was no way he could protect Waylynn from the heat. He didn't have any other choice. The water lapped at her mouth and nose. She gasped for air, pressing her palms against the container wall.

They were out of time.

Elliot set the flare against the lid. Plastic instantly melted then cooled in the freezing water, but within seconds left a hole wide enough for him to reach his hand through. The clear coffin immediately filled with water, submerging Waylynn completely. He shoved his hand inside the crude hole and ripped the lid from the box.

She was free.

Hauling her into him, he ignored the protest of his body and pumped his arms and legs hard for the surface. But he'd already lost too much blood. His lungs burned with the need for air. No. He'd just gotten her free from Henson's crude coffin. He wasn't going to let his body be the thing keeping her from staying alive now. His grip lightened on Waylynn and she slipped out of his hand. He grew heavier as he struggled the last five feet toward the surface.

Someone—Kate?—gripped under his arm and pushed him above water. Another gasp reached his ears. Waylynn. Relief flooded through him as Kate helped them maneuver around burning debris toward the dock. Sullivan, Elizabeth and Vincent each bent down to pull them from the water. His back hit the old wood and his breath wheezed from his lungs, momentarily cutting off his air supply and leaving him dizzy. "Let's never do that again."

Waylynn set her cheek against the dock, blue eyes heavy, skin pale. She wouldn't look at him, but it didn't matter. She was alive.

Movement registered out of the corner of his eye near the remnants of Blake Henson's boat. A hand slapped onto the dock, soaking wet, followed by the rest of the SOB who'd taken Waylynn from him.

"There's blood on her clothing." Elliot pushed to his feet, his steps unbalanced. He forced his feet to move, then again, his strength returning in small increments as oxygen filled his bloodstream. "Have her checked out. And if anything else happens to her, I'll put my files on every single one of you to good use."

Vincent hauled Kate's oxygen tank off her shoulders. "What files?"

Waylynn huddled beneath the blanket Sullivan wrapped around her. "Wh-w-where're you going?"

"There's something I need to finish." He tracked Henson onto what remained of the boat. The bastard better have a weapon stashed down below. He was going to need it. Elliot stepped onto the burning deck, his target straight ahead. "Permission to come aboard, Counselor."

GUNSHOT WOUND TO her arm. Mild hypothermia from nearly drowning in the ocean. Days of emotional havoc. Waylynn fisted the blanket one of the men on Elliot's team had provided for her as she waited to be cleared to leave in the back of the ambulance. Paramedics had pulled the bullet from her arm, stitched her up and stabilized her stats. She'd live, but her attacker? He had no idea what kind of violence she'd caged for the last fifteen years. But she'd show him.

A single officer escorted Blake Henson down the dock in cuffs.

Now was her chance.

She dumped the blanket onto the floor and slid from the back of the ambulance. The fishing knife she'd picked up after the Blackhawk Security team pulled her from the water warmed in her hand. No. Henson didn't get to waste away behind bars for the rest of his life. He was going to know exactly what kind of terror he'd put her through the last five days. Even if police apprehended her afterward, her lawyer had already taken everything from her. She had nothing left to lose. She was the only one who could make him pay.

A monster to destroy a monster.

A calloused hand wrapped around hers and the knife, his mouth pressed against her ear. Salt and humidity filled her lungs, his clothing still damp against her arm. "Never considered you the stabby type, Doc."

"Let go of me." Waylynn tried to pull her hand free. Heat burned through her veins as the officer forced Blake Henson into the back of a black-and-white cruiser. The man who'd destroyed her life stared right at her, a small curve to his mouth as the door slammed behind him. Hollowness settled in the pit of her stomach. She snapped her gaze to Elliot's, felt a pull at the sight of those mesmerizing gray eyes. She struggled to wrench out of his reach, the base of the blade cutting into her hand, he held it so tight. The cruiser pulled away and everything inside her went cold. Colder than the ocean the lawyer had left her to drown in. She turned on Elliot, shoving her uninjured hand against his chest. "Why did you stop me? I could've ended this for good."

Blake Henson was on retainer for one of the top genetics labs in the country, which meant he was a damn good lawyer. Genism Corporation hired only the best. Even if he defended himself during the trial, there was a chance he'd be free within months. The attorney blamed her for ruining his life.

She might not survive the next time he came after her.

Elliot held strong despite the leg injury he'd endured trying to save her life. Blood still soaked through his jeans and her shirt, a violent reminder of the night's events. His expression hardened, but his grip on her wrist lightened. "You're not a killer, Waylynn."

She froze. He wasn't serious, was he? Her skin felt too tight for her body under the weight of his attention. Red and blue patrol lights softened the edge to his expression but weren't enough to change her mind about him. "That's funny coming from you, because the last time we spoke, you called me a monster, you practically accused me of murdering my father and said you'd never trust me again."

"I was wrong." His fingertips traced the vein leading from the oversensitized skin of her wrist upward and a shiver, one that had nothing to do with the dropping temperature, chased down her spine. "About all of it. I'm sorry."

"You're sorry." Waylynn pried her wrist out of his hand, severing contact between them. "You took my biggest fear I believed about myself and you used it against me, Elliot. You hurt me deeper than anyone ever has before, deeper than when my father turned on me and my mother. I trusted you. You were my best friend, the only person I counted on to keep me safe. I... I loved you. But that wasn't enough, was it?" The cold that'd taken residence in her muscles reached her heart.

It took everything in her to turn around and head for Officer Ramsey waiting by her police cruiser. Her apartment wouldn't be the same, wouldn't give her solace like it did before she'd found Alexis Jacobs in her bathtub, but she couldn't stay here. Couldn't face him again—

"I'm not done with you, Doc." His fingers slipped around her arm, twisting her into him. Flecks of ice speckled his hair and beard from his dive into the ocean after her. Tension strained the cords between his shoulders and neck, and the memories of their twenty-four hours spent in passion flashed before her eyes.

She'd hired Blackhawk Security—hired him—to protect her. She owed him her life. She would've died in that coffin if he and his team hadn't intervened, but that had been their job. And none of that changed the fact he'd accused her of murder. Her. The woman he'd contemplated a future with, the woman he'd said he'd take a bullet for. Waylynn set her hand against his chest and closed her eyes to count off his heart rate.

One year. That was all it'd taken to fall in love with him. The beers after work, the '90s country battles, the slow sway of his body against hers outside her assistant's apartment after they'd searched it for evidence Anchorage PD might've missed. Each and every single one of them shredded through her now. She'd given him everything, risked telling him her deepest, darkest secret for the glimpse of a normal life. With him. And he'd thrown it in her face.

"Thank you for saving my life. Three times." Somehow, even after all the tears she'd shed over the past few hours, her lower lash line burned. But she wouldn't let them fall this time. She was stronger than that. Her heart lurched in her chest. He might not be done with her, but she'd made her decision. She opened her eyes, pressed him away. She was done with him. "I warned you about the people you push away, Elliot. Not all of them come back. Have Sullivan send me the invoice for your services. Then you can be free of me."

Turning her back to him was one of the hardest things she'd ever done in her life. It'd be so easy to forgive him. So easy to bury herself in his muscled arms. So easy to forget everything that'd happened the last five days. But what they'd had together had been a fantasy. Because no matter how close she'd come to death, she was the same person. And so was he.

She'd kept Officer Ramsey waiting long enough. Waylynn forced one foot in front of the other, heading toward the officer's cruiser.

"I don't care if you killed your father," he said.

Panic flared as she studied the crime scene techs and officers around them. "Why don't you say that louder? I don't think the entire police department heard you."

"I had Vincent run the prints on the gun, but I don't care what the report says. I don't care if you turn into a completely different person down the line because of your genetic makeup or if you don't want to leave Anchorage." Warmth slid down her spine as he closed the distance between them. She stepped back, but he only countered her move until her back hit the side of the ambulance. Elliot leveraged one arm above her head and leaned in, his mouth mere centimeters from hers. "I want to wake up to your face every morning and go to bed with you every night. I want to binge-eat peanut-butter Oreos until we're both sick to our stomachs and greet you with a beer after you come home from work. I want to see how much you know about country after the '90s. I want you, Doc. Since the moment I laid eyes on you that day I moved next door, I've wanted you. And I will do anything to make you mine."

His mouth crashed down on hers, his tongue sweeping past her lips to claim her. And she let him. Just like that first time he'd kissed her outside her apartment. One brush of his teeth against her bottom lip and she tumbled head over heels into intoxication. And she could almost forget the fact he'd called her a monster, or that he'd been collecting files on everyone he claimed he cared about.

The pain in her hand intensified as her fingers constricted around the fishing knife. Reality barged through her system and Waylynn ripped away. Escaping from the feel of him pressed against her, she gulped freezing oxygen to clear her head. "I can't do this."

"Here? Because I'm happy to do it somewhere else," he said. "My SUV's over—"

"No. This. Us." She motioned between them. "It's not that you called me a monster, Elliot. I've known what I am—what I might become—for years and have come to terms with it. It's that you said it right after we started talking about a future together. You needed a way out."

The sarcasm in his gaze disappeared. "A way out?"

"You keep blackmail files on the people you rely on to have your back. You're so determined to keep everyone at a distance with your jokes, you never let anyone in because you're afraid they might turn on you." And he had good reason. She shook her head, folding her arms across her midsection in an effort to keep the tremors at bay. "It couldn't have been easy growing up the way you did or easy behind bars after you were arrested in Iraq, but you're not in prison anymore. You're not supposed to look for a way out of the relationships you claim you care about, and I don't want to wake up one morning and find your side of the bed empty, Elliot. And until you realize some people—like the ones on your team—are worth hanging on to… I can't be part of your life anymore. So here it is. Here's your way out."

Elliot ran his palms down his face, the bloodstains on his clothing shifting in the newness of morning light. Tears welled in his eyes, but he refused to look at her. "Who's going to drink all my beer after work every night?"

"I don't know." Her insides shattered. She couldn't

swallow around the lump in her throat. Couldn't breathe. Waylynn headed for Officer Ramsey's patrol car, determined more than ever not to look back. Tossing the fisherman's knife across the marina parking lot, she curled her hand around the thin cut across her palm as she walked. "But it can't be me."

Chapter Fifteen

Three days later...

An ear-piercing scream had Elliot reaching for the gun stashed under his pillow. He threw back the sheets and shoved out of bed, not bothering to check the time as the apartment blurred in his vision. He'd made it halfway to the front door before he slowed.

Damn it. Third night in the last three days.

Setting his forehead against the nearest wall, he forced his pulse rate to slow. He dropped the gun to his side. No matter how much he wanted to bust down her front door and chase back the nightmares she suffered from since Blake Henson had tried to drown her in the ocean, Waylynn had made herself perfectly clear. They weren't friends anymore.

He slammed the butt of the gun into the wall. Once. Twice. A growl ripped from his throat, but he forced himself to hide the gun back under his pillow. He might as well start the investigation for his new client. There was no way he'd be getting back to sleep. Not when he knew she was on the other side of the wall, scared, suffering. Alone.

"Hell." What he wouldn't give to drag her back to the cabin, make her forget everything that'd happened. Take back what he'd said, prove he didn't have a backup plan when it came to her. Swiping his hand down his face, he hauled his stupid ass to the kitchen and started the coffeemaker. He opened his laptop and took a seat at the bar, the glow from the screen lighting the rest of the kitchen and living room.

His attention immediately went to the only file folder on the desktop, the one Waylynn had broken into somehow. He entered in his password, the title of her favorite '90s country song, and hit Enter. The file exploded into separate documents, photos and research. Jane Reise, Sullivan's army prosecutor. Anthony Harris. Elizabeth Dawson. Kate Monroe and the intel he'd gathered from the attack on her and her husband last year. The rest of the Blackhawk Security team and then some. Every secret, every lie, every trace of his targets' existence was in these files. He scrubbed his hands down his face. "I hate it when she's right."

Which was often.

Every piece of intel he'd gathered over the last year and stored in this file had been leverage. A reason to distance himself from the people he claimed to care about, just as she'd said. His fingers brushed the small black-and-red thumb drive Kate had recovered from the side of the road. As far as he knew,

Waylynn's father's police report was still stored on the device. Along with the research she'd tried to recover before her Genism access had been cut off.

He plugged the drive into the side of his laptop and waited as it loaded. There. At the bottom of the search window. He positioned the mouse over the Nathan Hargraves police report and dragged it into the virtual trash bin. Then he did the same with every single file he'd collected on his team, on his neighbors, on anyone whom he hadn't been assigned to investigate. Except one.

No, he'd keep that one. Because Kate Monroe deserved to know the truth about what happened to her husband. Printing off the pages from that particular file, he dressed quickly, then ejected the storage drive and grabbed the overnight bag he'd hung on to since the night he'd pulled Waylynn from the bottom of the ocean.

The sudden glow of his phone from the couch where he'd tossed it ripped him back. The team had been trying to reach him for three days. Amazing the thing still had a charge after so many damn calls. Scooping the device from the cushion, he answered. "Make it fast."

"Answer the door, Dunham," Vincent demanded.

Three knocks twisted him toward the front door. He disconnected and discarded the phone, rolling back his injured shoulder as he unlocked the dead bolt. Vincent Kalani stood on the other side. Falling back against the door, Elliot ushered the forensics expert inside, but the rigidity and tension in the man's body language announced his intentions before Vincent opened his mouth.

"I didn't steal your lunch if that's why you're here." Elliot closed the door, then set Waylynn's overnight bag onto the couch. He'd been about to break her door down if she didn't answer. This wasn't over. Not by a long shot.

"Ugh. You sound so depressed it makes me cringe. I wish you would've answered your phone so I didn't have to see your face." The massive former cop handed him a manila file folder. "Thought you might want to see this."

Elliot took the folder with the single sheet of paper inside. Black smudges and a hell of a lot of technical terms stared up at him, but it wasn't hard to understand what was inside. "The fingerprints on the gun aren't Waylynn's."

"Your girl didn't kill her father after all. Fingerprints came back as Nora Hargraves. Her mother." Vincent Kalani studied the small apartment. "You know, some color would really brighten up this dark, sad cave of an existence you've decided to live."

He couldn't focus on the forensic expert's usual insults. He stared at the report. Read it again. And again. Waylynn had been protecting her mother all these years. "Where's the gun?"

"The blood on the woman's shirt belonged to the father. Wife must've been wearing it when she pulled the trigger." Vincent dived into his leather jacket pocket and pulled an evidence bag free, handing the gun that'd killed Nathan Hargraves over. "Case is officially closed."

The weight of the gun kept him grounded. Wouldn't have mattered what the report said either way but knowing Waylynn had been protecting her ill mother all this time only made him love her more. "Will Waylynn be charged with tampering with the evidence?"

"Not unless someone turns her in." Vincent circled around him toward the door. The former NYPD officer reached for the door but turned back. "Back at the docks, you said something about using files against us if something happened to her. You got one on me?"

"Not anymore," he said.

"Good." Vincent swung the door open. "I was afraid I'd have to kill you."

A short scoff escaped his mouth as his teammate closed the door behind him. Elliot had no doubt the forensics expert would follow through, too. As a former cop, Vincent Kalani had embedded himself with some of the evilest kinds of people in New York City. People who could destroy lives if they discovered Vincent had been a cop the whole time. But, the man's secrets were safe with Elliot. Always would be.

And so would Waylynn's.

Because he cared, damn it. About her. She was the person worth risking his own happiness for, the one he couldn't spend the rest of his life without. He grabbed her overnight bag and shoved the flash drive she'd stored her research on and the gun inside. Cool morning air slammed into him as he nearly ripped the front door off its hinges and pivoted in front of her door. Her apartment had been cleared as a crime scene, but pieces of police tape fluttered in the small breeze. He knocked, ready to face his future.

With her.

The door opened, the sight on the other side more than his lungs could bear.

She answered the door and all the reasons he'd thought of to keep his distance from her disappeared. A wavy waterfall of blond hair framed the healing bruises along one side of her jaw and skimmed across her collarbones. Those ocean-blue eyes narrowed on him, the same color as the sling wrapping her left arm. She was everything he'd dreamed of and more. Intelligent, sexy, defiant and strong. And, hell, he wasn't good enough for her.

"Elliot? What are you doing here?" Waylynn tried folding her uninjured arm across her chest, gaze locking on the bag in his hand as she shifted her weight onto one foot. Surprise smoothed the edges of her full mouth, but she didn't move to take her stuff from him. "If you came here to apologize—"

"I wanted to bring back your stuff. The flash drive's in there, along with my MIT shirt you like so much. Kate collected all your things from the side of the highway after…" He offered her the bag to distract himself from the rage burning through him at the thought of that night. "After you'd disappeared. The gun, too."

"Oh." Her mouth parted, hand relaxing down to her side right before she reached out to take the bag from him. "I thought Vincent was running prints on it."

"He did." But the results didn't matter. He knew the truth. The woman standing in front of him wasn't a killer, wasn't a monster.

"So you know who killed my father, then." Dropping the bag beside the door, she rested her weight against it but didn't move to slam the door in his face. Progress. "Are you going to turn me in for keeping the evidence all these years?"

"No." The statute of limitations was still in effect, but he wouldn't have said a damn word even if it wasn't. "I know you were protecting your mom so she didn't have to spend her last days behind bars. I don't blame you. If you can believe it, it only made me fall harder for you. What I don't understand is why you couldn't tell me the truth. Why keep protecting her after she's gone?"

Her shoulders rose on a strong inhale.

"My mother was a good woman. I wanted her to be remembered that way. Not as a killer. And… I was afraid you'd have me arrested for tampering with the murder weapon." A weak smile played across her mouth, homing his focus to her lips. "Thank you for bringing back my things. But if the police do find out, I don't expect you to lie for me—"

"I deleted all the files I had on my team and your father's police report." He pushed his hands into his jeans. Silence stretched between them for a moment. "You were right. I've been looking for a way out of a lot of situations in my life. My debt to Sullivan, the relationships I have with my team. What I had with you." Rolling an invisible rock on the cement with his boot, he lowered his attention to her perfectly painted red toenails and smiled. "I thought my twisted sense of freedom was the most important contributor to my happiness, but I was wrong." He raised his gaze to hers. "You make me happy, Doc, and if nothing else, I want things to go back the way they were. The thought of losing you completely guts me from the inside, but I'll be happy just to be your friend again. If you'll let me."

Her hand slipped down the edge of the door. "It's not like you to give up."

"I'm not giving up." It was the truth. He'd fight to stay in her life, even if he couldn't have her for himself, and he'd spend the rest of his life trying to make her happy in return. "You're selfless, you're kind, you put others first and will go out of your way to protect the ones you care about, even if you're the one to take the fall. You deserve someone worthy of all those things, Doc. You deserve someone as good as you. You deserve someone better than me and I'm sorry."

"Yeah." She fisted her fingers in his T-shirt and pulled him over the threshold of her apartment.

Notching her head higher, she leveled her mouth with his. Her geranium scent filled his lungs with every breath as his heart threatened to beat out of his chest. "You're probably right, but where's the fun in that?"

EVERYBODY HAD AN ADDICTION. Hers just happened to be him.

Need bubbled beneath her skin, moving and flowing as thick as molten lava. And if she wasn't careful, she'd erupt all over the damn place. Hot. Destructive. Unforgiving.

Waylynn kissed him—hard, fast, trying to quench the desire for him she'd ignored for the last three days. Every second without him had been agony. Every night waking up alone from her nightmares had torn her apart a little bit more. She dragged him inside and used her foot to close the door behind them, all the while never taking her mouth off his. Happiness throttled through her unlike anything she'd experienced before. Her hand shook as she framed his jawline and pulled back to catch her breath.

Her skin tingled where he touched her, her nerve endings on fire. For him. He'd risked his life for her, given up his most valuable possession for the chance to be with her. His willingness to try to make this work between them deepened the ache behind her sternum. "What's it like not having a backup plan for once?"

"Not sure yet. I literally deleted the files ten minutes ago. Still hasn't sunk in, but I can tell you the time I took to put them together is now free." His eyebrows bounced on his forehead and she couldn't stop the laugh forcing its way up her throat. "I should tell you I kept one file."

Vulnerability claimed her, and she sank flat on her feet from her toes as she stared up at him. Her hand slipped to his shoulder, careful to avoid the bullet wound on one side. "What file?"

"Kate's," he said.

"Are you going to tell her the truth?"

"I have to. She could still be in danger." Elliot ran a hand through his hair, clearly affected by the event. "She thinks it's over."

Kate had helped save her from Blake Henson's clear coffin at the bottom of the ocean. All this time, the team's psychologist had kept it together after losing the most important person in her life. How? "She deserves to know."

"Nobody knows outside of the team." He held her a bit tighter, reflecting the growing need inside her to keep him as close as possible. Because if she lost him again… No. She couldn't think like that. Couldn't imagine a life without him in it. Didn't want to. "I didn't tell you I was the one who looked into it after the ambush happened and found the shooter a few days later. He'd been off his meds for a while and I got him the help he needed in a hospital."

"Then why keep the file?" she asked.

"Kate needs to know what really went down that

night." Elliot threaded his fingers into her hair at the base of her neck. "If something like that had ever happened to you, I'd want to know the truth."

"Then you should tell her." She nodded. "Just, however you do it, remind her you're the messenger and don't get yourself killed in the process, okay? I almost lost you once. I'm not about to let it happen again."

He buried his nose in her neck and inhaled deep. Elliot squeezed her tight until air pressurized in her lungs, but she didn't dare push away. Lifting his head, he brushed a strand of hair out of her face and tucked it behind her ear. Electric jolts speared through her, her insides, down to her bones as he locked those mesmerizing gray eyes on her. No one had ever looked at her as he did. Like she was important. Like he needed her to breathe. "Careful, Doc, you're starting to make me think you care about me."

"Maybe a little." Her lips spread thin in a wide smile. "I mean you're the only one who knows my secrets. Kind of freeing in a way. I'd like to hang on to that feeling for a while."

"Oh, is that all I'm good for?" Elliot slipped his hands to her waist, swaying them back and forth in a slow rhythm. Taking her uninjured hand, he extended it out away from them and swung her to one side. He set his mouth against her ear as they danced in the middle of her living room, one hand pressed against the small of her back, the other tightening in hers. Thoughts of their first dance outside this very apartment pulled her deeper. "I'll take it. I'll take anything I can get from you for the rest of our lives, but you're going to have to tell me why you have moving boxes all over your apartment sooner or later."

"Aren't you a private investigator?" She studied her living room and the dozens of open boxes, rolls of packing tape and labels. This apartment had once been a safe haven, somewhere she could get away from the demands of her job and binge on peanut butter Oreos and her favorite TV shows as long as she wanted. All the while knowing her best friend lived next door. "Or was kissing me too much of a distraction?"

A deep laugh rumbled through him and she reveled in the vibration running through her body. "You think highly of yourself, don't you?"

"I'm going to be honest. I haven't showered in two days because I can't stand the thought of going back in that bathroom. I've been brushing my teeth over the kitchen sink. It doesn't feel the same as it did before." The images ingrained in her head when she'd found Alexis would stay with her for the rest of her life. And she couldn't stay here anymore. Nerves fired through her as she turned back to him and she licked the dryness from her lips. "So... I bought a place. I'm moving in two days, but it'd be nice to have a bodyguard living with me in case someone else at my company decides to kill me."

"Why, Dr. Hargraves, are you asking me to move

in with you?" He stopped swaying, pulled her closer. A brightness in his eyes speared straight through her, filling her with hope, chasing back the darkness that made up her DNA. "Are you sure that's a good idea considering your Dr. Jekyll, Ms. Hyde situation?"

"You've already taken down one monster." She refused to let the events of the last week encroach on this moment and slipped her fingers over the gauze taped to his shoulder. "I think you're up for the challenge."

"You're not a monster, Waylynn." He notched her chin higher and forced her to look at him, all sarcasm, all joking leaving his voice. "You're the kindest, sexiest woman I've ever met and nothing in this world will ever convince me otherwise. Besides, if it turns out you are, I could chain you to the bed, right?"

A wide grin deepened the lines at the edges of his mouth.

"You could try." A soft laugh escaped her throat as she closed her eyes and set her ear over his chest. The strong beat of his pulse kept rhythm with hers, as though they were the same body, the same soul, and she never wanted to move. Except the movers would force her to when they came to load her boxes onto the truck.

"No matter what happens, we're in this together," he said. "I was stupid to push you away. I love you, Doc, and I will prove it to you every day of our lives to make it up to you if I have to."

"Yes, you were, but I still love you. Always have. Always will." The nightmare was over. Officer Ramsey had informed her Blake Henson would serve life behind bars for the murder of her assistant and for his stunt trying to drown her in the ocean. The board had overturned Dr. Stover's decision to let her go and she was free to return to work as soon as she was ready. With a promotion and a raise, considering the events of the past couple of weeks. But maybe taking her work to a different lab wouldn't be the worst thing in the world. As long as Elliot came with her.

Waylynn pulled his mouth to hers and lost herself in him all over again. Would she ever get used to the way he affected her? His clean, masculine scent dived deep into her lungs and sealed the deal. No. Never. He was hers. No matter what happened from here on out, they were in it together. Forever. "Now help me with these boxes. They're not going to pack themselves."

Most important, she had Elliot.

Her best friend. Her bodyguard. Her everything.

Epilogue

Kate Monroe pulled two photo frames from the box and arranged them on her desk in her office, skimming her thumb over the glass. The team had left everything the same since she'd taken her leave, but couldn't they have at least watered the plants?

Three knocks on her door snapped her head up.

Elliot Dunham stood in the doorway, a manila file folder in his hand. The cocky private investigator always had a smile on his face these days. One of the upsides to being in love, and her heart panged. Not out of jealousy. Out of admiration. "Looking good, Monroe."

"Thanks. Glad to see you back, too." She shuffled the paperwork from her last case for Blackhawk Security to a corner on her desk as a distraction. The case had been assigned to her a year ago. Before... She stopped that thought in its track. She'd have to look into that one and see what became of the profile she'd written for Vincent. "How's your life? Does Waylynn need—"

"No, thank you. She's great. Other than she still has nightmares a couple times a week." Hesitation deepened the lines in his forehead as he moved fully into the office. "But she's not why I'm here."

Confusion slithered through her. Elliot hadn't been assigned any new cases as far as she knew. He wasn't supposed to be back in the office until next week. "Do you need a profile?"

"Actually, I'm here because of you." He tossed the folder onto her desk, the sharp corner hitting the back of her hand. The label spelled out her name and she narrowed her attention on him. What was this? "I'm here because your husband is alive, Kate."

* * * * *

Look for Nichole Severn's next
Harlequin Intrigue, Rules in Surrender.
Read on for a sneak peek.

Your husband is alive, Kate.

Blackhawk Security profiler Kate Monroe stared at her reflection in the broken picture frame on the floor. Had it really been an entire year? She hadn't set foot in this house since the ambush, too traumatized to pull the bullets out of the walls, too sentimental to put it on the market. Everything had changed that night. Tightening her grip on the manila file folder in her hand, she couldn't ignore the truth. Declan hadn't died as she'd been told while recovering in the hospital from her own injuries. He'd survived. He'd disappeared. And he'd left her behind.

Glass crunched under her shoes, bringing her back to the moment, and the photo came into focus. Her and Declan dancing at their wedding, surrounded by smiling guests. Burying the burn behind her sternum deeper, she stepped over the frame. Blackhawk's private investigator had found proof—a time-stamped photo—of Declan taken a month ago in downtown Anchorage. She'd stared at it for hours, picked it apart pixel by pixel to fight the anger and resentment bubbling up her throat. In vain. The photo was real. Declan was alive and she deserved to know why he hadn't come home.

There had to be something here that would lead her to his location. Setting the file on what was left of the kitchen table, she fought back the memories of hundreds of dinners as she dragged her fingers over the bullet-ridden surface. She pulled out drawers in the kitchen, emptied the bookshelf beside the desk Declan had built for her, scattered old patient files across the carpet. Bending to pick them up, Kate froze as the dark stains at her feet came into focus. Blood. Ice worked through her. She couldn't think. Couldn't breathe. She closed her eyes against the memories fighting to rush forward and forced herself to take a deep breath. She'd been a psychologist. She'd helped others through their trauma, their pain—why couldn't she get past her own?

She traced over one mound of scar tissue below her collarbone, leaving the files where they fell. Swallowing against the tightness in her throat, she straightened. Gunshot wounds never healed. Not really. Six months since the last surgery and the physical pain from three shots to the chest hadn't lessened. Then again, she'd been lucky to survive at all. The gunman who'd opened fire on her and Declan hadn't meant to leave anyone alive.

Movement registered off to her right, and she automatically reached for the Glock in her shoulder holster. Depressing the safety tab, she took aim, heart in her throat. Blackhawk Security's founder and CEO insisted his agents trained in wilderness survival, weapons, hostage negotiation, recovery and rescue, and more, but she was a profiler. Not former military like Anthony. Not a former NSA consultant like Elizabeth. She'd never had use for a gun. Her hands shook slightly as the weight of it threatened to pull her arms down. She'd never aimed her gun at another human being.

"You're trespassing on private property. Come out with your hands where I can see them, and I promise not to shoot you."

The house had been abandoned for a year. Wasn't hard to imagine the homeless taking advantage of a roof over their heads, and she wasn't interested in forcing them to leave if that was the case. The house wasn't going anywhere. It took everything she had to stay here this long.

Shadows shifted across the intruder's features, and her breath caught in her throat. Hints of moonlight highlighted the familiar shape of his stubbled jaw, his broad chest, muscled arms and short blond hair. Her heart beat hard behind her sternum as she stood there, unsure if he was real or a figment of her imagination. He closed the distance between them, slowly, cautiously, as though he believed she might actually shoot him. She couldn't make out the color of his eyes in the darkness but pictured the ice-blue depths clearly from memory as he stared back at her.

"It's you."

She suppressed the sob clawing up her throat but couldn't fight the burn in her lower lash line. Rushing forward, Kate wrapped her arms around his broad chest, his clean masculine scent working deep into her lungs.

A year. A year he'd put her through hell. The grief, the anger. Why hadn't he reached out to her? Who had she buried all those months ago? Why wasn't he hugging her back? Clenching her back teeth to keep the scream at bay, Kate backed off but didn't holster the weapon. Why was he just standing there? "Say something."

"You're even more beautiful than I remembered." That voice. His voice. An electric sizzle caught her nerve endings on fire and exploded throughout her entire system. She'd never thought she'd hear that voice again. Declan Monroe shifted closer, the weight of his gaze pressurizing the air in her lungs. "You don't need the gun. I'm not going to hurt you."

"That's all you're going to say to me?" It felt as if someone had driven a fist into her stomach. "You've been alive this whole time, and that's all you're going to say? They told me you died in that hospital. I—" The pain of that day, of losing her best friend, of losing the man she'd intended to spend the rest of her life with, the man she'd planned on starting a family with, surged to the surface. "I buried you."

"I can't imagine what you've been through." He reached out, smoothed his fingertips down her jawline. Even with the ice of shock coursing through her veins, warmth penetrated deep into her bones, but his expression kept her from reveling in his missed touch.

Declan lowered his hand as he studied the aftermath of the living room. The pockmarked walls, the broken picture frames, the destroyed sectional and cushions. She didn't have the guts to see what'd become of the rest of the house, a home that'd once been their safe haven from their dark careers. "Is this where it happened?"

Confusion gripped her hard, and Kate narrowed her eyes to see his face clearly. "What do you mean—"

"I get these flashes sometimes. Of this house, of different things." Declan motioned to his head then his gaze locked back on her. "Mostly of you. Some days it's glimpses, other times I can see you so clearly walking through that front door with stacks of files in your arms and a smile on your face. Like it was real."

Her head jerked slightly to the side of its own accord as though she'd been slapped. Instinct screamed this wasn't right, and she took a step back, the gun still in her hand.

"But I still don't know your name," he said.

Air rushed from her lungs. She struggled to keep upright as the world tilted on its axis. Strong hands steadied her before she hit the blood-stained floor a second time, but the gun slipped from her hold.

Leveraging her weight against the desk, she pushed back stray hairs that'd escaped from the low bun at the base of her neck. She had to breathe. Her pulse beat hard at the base of her throat as his hand slipped down her spine. How could he have forgotten her name? Every cell in her body rejected the idea her husband had been walking around Anchorage without the slightest clue he'd been married, had a life, had a job. Where had he been all this time?

"You okay?" He was still touching her. Even through the thick fabric of her cargo jacket, she recognized those familiar strokes. "I'll get you some water."

"No." The city had probably turned off the water a long time ago. She'd been paying the mortgage on the house in addition to the rent on her small apartment, but utilities would've been a waste. Kate maneuvered out of his reach. "I'm fine. I…need some air."

Lie. Nothing about the situation, about the fact the husband she'd lost was standing in front of her, was fine. And fresh air wouldn't do a damn bit of good. Space. She needed space. The home they'd shared for more than half a decade blurred in her peripheral vision as she headed for the front door. Debris and remnants of their life together threatened to trip her up, but she wouldn't stop until there were at least two inches of door between them. Couldn't.

The cold Alaskan night prickled goose bumps along her arms as she closed the door behind her. She set the crown of her head against the wood, pressing her shoulders into the door. One breath. Two. None of this made sense. His surgeon had told her Declan hadn't survived the shooting. That he'd done everything he could to save her husband, but nothing worked. Declan had lost too much blood, the bullets had torn through major arteries and nobody could've saved him.

No wonder he'd suggested she take the time to heal from her own wounds before identifying the body. It hadn't been to save her from seeing her husband on a slab. It'd been to cover his mistake. By the time she'd had the strength to get out of that damn bed, it'd been too late. The hospital had released who she thought had been her husband into her custody, and Declan's former partner had taken responsibility for all of the funeral arrangements. Nobody knew her husband hadn't been inside that coffin?

The surgeon had lied. Why?

She swiped at her face as the tears finally fell. Declan didn't know her name?

Tires screeched on asphalt a few houses down. Headlights flared to life, but she couldn't see the driver through the truck's windshield. Probably one of the neighbor's teenagers. It'd been so long since she'd lived on the street, she didn't know who'd moved away after the shooting, her neighbor's names or if any of them had kids old enough to drive. Wasn't important. Staying calm long enough to assess the situation—that was all that mattered now. The engine revved loud in her ears as the faint outline of the passenger-side window lowered.

The door supporting her disappeared, strong hands pulling her inside a split second before the first bullet of many shattered through the house's main window. Kate hit the floor hard, her head snapping back as Declan returned fire. She checked her holster—empty—and recognized the gun in his hand. Her Glock.

The sound of peeling tires faded, and the gunfire ceased.

Declan barricaded them inside the house, back to the front door as he dropped the gun's magazine, counted the rounds and slammed it back into place. Guess there were some things amnesia couldn't destroy. Loading a weapon being one of them. Light blue eyes settled on her as he offered her his hand. Calluses slid against her palms as he wrapped his hand around hers and pulled her into him. "Are you hurt?"

"I'm getting tired of people shooting at me." Her awareness of him hiked to an all-time high. The pounding of his heart beat against her palm, the pressure of his attention on her. Even the way he held her took a bit of the strength out of her knees. She shook her head and stepped out of his reach to counteract the heat rising in her neck. He'd saved her life. The least she could do was help him recover his. "It's Kate, by the way. My name is Kate."

WE HOPE YOU ENJOYED THIS BOOK!

HARLEQUIN®

INTRIGUE

Dive into action-packed suspense.
Solve crimes. Pursue justice.

Look for six new books available every
month, wherever books are sold!

Harlequin.com

AVAILABLE THIS MONTH FROM
Harlequin Intrigue®

SAFETY BREACH
Longview Ridge Ranch • by Delores Fossen

Former profiler Gemma Hanson is in witness protection, but she's still haunted by memories of the serial killer who tried to kill her last year. Her concerns skyrocket when Sheriff Kellan Slater tells her the murderer has learned her location and is coming to finish what he started.

UNDERCOVER ACCOMPLICE
Red, White and Built: Delta Force Deliverance
by Carol Ericson

When Delta Force soldier Hunter Mancini learns the group that kidnapped CIA operative Sue Chandler is now framing his team leader, he asks for her help. But could she be hiding something that would clear his boss?

AMBUSHED AT CHRISTMAS
Rushing Creek Crime Spree • by Barb Han

After a jogger resembling Detective Leah Cordon is murdered, rancher Deacon Kent approaches her, believing the attack is related to recent cattle mutilations. Can they find the killer before he corners Leah?

DANGEROUS CONDITIONS
Protectors at Heart • by Jenna Kernan

Former soldier Logan Lynch's first investigation as the constable of a small town leads him to microbiologist Paige Morris, whose boss was killed. Yet as they search for the murderer, Paige is forced to reveal a secret that shows the stakes couldn't be higher.

RULES IN DEFIANCE
Blackhawk Security • by Nichole Severn

Blackhawk Security investigator Elliot Dunham never expected his neighbor to show up bruised and covered in blood in the middle of the night. To protect Waylynn Hargraves, Elliot must defy the rules he's set for himself, because he knows he's all that stands between her and certain death.

HIDDEN TRUTH
Stealth • by Danica Winters

When undercover CIA agent Trevor Martin meets Sabrina Parker, the housekeeper at the ranch where he's lying low, he doesn't know she's an undercover FBI agent. After a murder on the property, the operatives must work together, but can they discover their hidden connection before it's too late?

LOOK FOR THESE AND OTHER HARLEQUIN INTRIGUE BOOKS WHEREVER BOOKS ARE SOLD, INCLUDING MOST BOOKSTORES, SUPERMARKETS, DISCOUNT STORES AND DRUGSTORES.

HIATMBPA1219